LAST QUADRANT

MEIRA CHAND

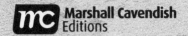
Marshall Cavendish
Editions

First published in 1981 by John Murray (Publishers) Ltd

This new edition published by Marshall Cavendish Editions in 2018
An imprint of Marshall Cavendish International

A member of the
Times Publishing Group

Other Marshall Cavendish Offices:
Marshall Cavendish Corporation. 99 White Plains Road, Tarrytown NY 10591-
9001, USA • Marshall Cavendish International (Thailand) Co Ltd. 253 Asoke,
12th Flr, Sukhumvit 21 Road, Klongtoey Nua, Wattana, Bangkok 10110, Thailand
• Marshall Cavendish (Malaysia) Sdn Bhd, Times Subang, Lot 46, Subang Hi-Tech
Industrial Park, Batu Tiga, 40000 Shah Alam, Selangor Darul Ehsan, Malaysia

Marshall Cavendish is a registered trademark of Times Publishing Limited

National Library Board, Singapore Cataloguing-in-Publication Data

Name(s): Chand, Meira.
Title: Last quadrant / Meira Chand.
Description: Singapore : Marshall Cavendish Editions, 2018. | First published:
John Murray (Publishers) Ltd, 1981.
Identifier(s): OCN 1037826463 | ISBN 978-981-48-2822-2 (paperback)
Subject(s): LCSH: Orphanages--Japan--Fiction. | Typhoons--Fiction. | Japan--
Fiction.
Classification: DDC 823.914--dc23

Printed in Singapore

Cover design by Lorraine Aw

For
Kumar

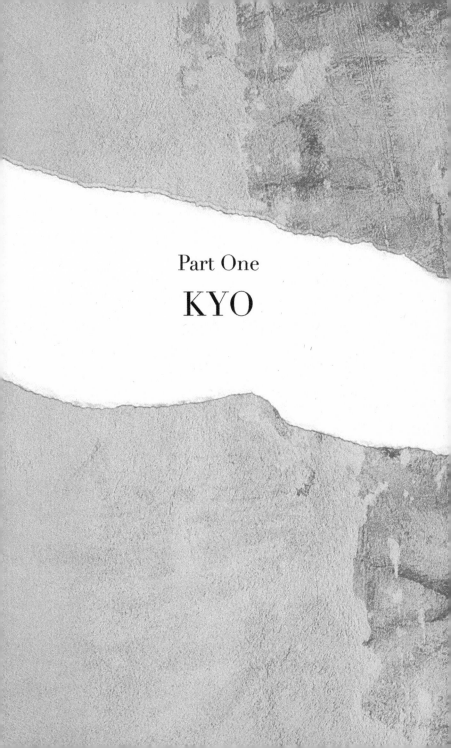

Part One
KYO

1. Thursday

'May I come in then?' Kyo asked. She had not waited at the outer gate, but let herself in and approached the front steps, as if such familiarity was in order. It was twenty years since Eva last saw her.

In the fierce light of the doorstep Kyo's small figure was bright and hard as a chip of stone. Eva blocked the passage with an arm before the open door. From behind came the odour of stewing bones from the soup she was preparing, a bald and fetid smell. Escaping the kitchen it seeped out about her into the sun of the garden and borders of marigolds. Their colours were deep and velvet against the parched dry beds of soil. Eva stared over the half moons of her glasses, and shock flushed in a cold dry burn.

Dropping her arm from the doorway, Eva moved a few inches back. Kyo's cheap perfume sharpened her nostrils, before the cooking bones engulfed it. The cloying film of make-up was thicker than before, the lips pulped and soft from that secret life Eva knew little of. But suddenly she remembered the fine texture of Kyo's skin, stretched over the wide flat planes of her face, scrubbed and shiny, free of make-up, on that first day Eva brought her to the orphanage, more than twenty-five years before. Now she thought, how changed she is, how old she has become; she must be forty-five.

Kyo followed Eva into the room but stopped at its carpeted threshold. 'Not a thing has changed.' She looked round in a deprecating way, and then stepped boldly forward.

Eva stood silently, one thought above all filling her head. Why has she come after all these years, when I thought of her as dead? Before her Kyo walked about, touching, appraising the small cramped room. Its frail oriental scale was unsuited to the Western adaption of carpets, chairs and tables. The reflective glass doors of the china cabinet mirrored Kyo's presence to her. Yes, Eva thought, the room was the same as when Kyo last saw it, except for the twenty years it contained.

Through those years Eva had continued to live on the hill, in charge of St Christopher's orphanage, and surrounded by the same neighbours. Some way further up the road resided the Englishman, Arthur John Wilcox. Far below, the fortress of the Coopers' house possessed the narrow sea road along the beach at Suma. From these predestined points upon the hill they consumed a com-mon view, of the Inland Sea of Japan and the town of Kobe on Osaka bay. They dissolved within the same sunset and watched the same unfolding day brim upon the sea. In a small house beside the orphanage Eva Kraig had lived all this time with her daughter, Akiko, adopted from the woman, Kyo Matsumoto. The years had passed between them smooth as glass, until this moment of Kyo's return.

And the thought of Akiko pressed dark and thick then in Eva's head. For she feared she knew why Kyo had come, all that she would say. She was thankful Akiko had gone that morning, earlier than usual, across to the orphanage. Whatever the reason Kyo had come, Eva wished to absorb it alone.

'Sit down,' she suggested.

Kyo sat with one leg crossing the other. A backless shoe gaped from her foot, a blue vein traced her heel. Beneath the make-up her flesh had the bloodlessness of plants shut away from sun. For she spent her life within a nocturnal warren of bars. Eva knew. She slept through the day, a drained whisky glass beside a stale bed. That was the life she had chosen, of the bars and a night-time world.

Head on one side Kyo lit a cigarette, inhaling with narrowed eyes. She looked deeply at Eva a moment, as if choosing an instant to strike. And Eva waited, cold and fixed, stiff with the twenty years behind that held at their core fear of this moment she knew was about to come. Sometimes she had dreamed of it, and woken. But the child was always there beside her, sleeping, peaceful, safe. Kyo exhaled smoke in a soft whistled breath. It meandered up in gossamer strands through a ray of light. Heat overwhelmed the room already warmed by the bald odour of the cooking soup bones. Eva wished for strength to open the window. But she sat, apprehensive and tense on a high-backed chair, her eyes on the golden sphere of carpet that ended the ray of light. Within it a threadbare warp pushed through a flowered border. Eva kept her eyes there and did not look up. She waited for the words.

'I want Akiko back.'

It was easier once she had heard them. She raised her head calmly, everything in her stilled. 'She's not yours to have back. You relinquished that claim. Easily, gratefully. Have you forgotten? Is it convenient again to become her mother? You know I adopted her legally.'

She knew then that the words had been buried within her through all the years behind, waiting, guarding against this moment. She held her breath and the words reverberated on, filling the room and her head. From the window the shaft of light, like a pale laser beam, divided the space between them. Behind the dusty shifting ray Kyo appeared untouchable.

Eva stood up. She pulled wide the curtains in a rush and clatter of hooks and threw up the window. At once the sinister beam dissolved in sun and the dry smell of hot soil rose from the garden. Beyond the window Eva glimpsed the glassy surface of the sea and the dark shape of Awaji island. That morning the heat was still and oppressive, as if the sky pressed it flat upon the earth. Summer still spread a net over Autumn, refusing to relinquish it.

Eva turned to face Kyo, her back to the window, and saw the woman defenceless. Kyo shaded her eyes against the light, hardness peeled from her face like the skin of a grape on the soft naked flesh beneath. And Eva saw again Kyo's face on a night she remembered so well, smashed and mobile then with terror. On the night Eva found her, battered, abandoned, flung into a dirty frozen gutter. Then she had taken the girl in her arms, wiped the bruising and blood. Remembering, pictures surged up, one after another, tumbling into her mind. She pushed them down, to concentrate on Akiko.

Akiko. Her daughter. She could not think of her as less. She could not think of her as Kyo's child. Already she was twenty-two, years had melted quickly. Often, since the time the child first came to her, they had walked together on the gritty strip of nearby beach, and Eva had seen their shadows mingled there in wet sand, holding hands. At her side the child's breath was almost her own, in frail shells they had listened for the sea. And at night the child's body, limp with sleep, hollowed her out with love. Akiko. Eva stiffened and looked coldly at Kyo's upturned face. Kyo was like bad flesh you cut away, or the rot of fallen fruit.

'I was ill ... I am ill ... it's bad. They told me they can't say anything. Maybe they'll cure me. I don't know. I can't think any more about it.' Kyo put a hand to her cheek. Eva saw fear and weariness, she saw the loneliness Kyo would never admit.

'I haven't lived in Japan for twenty years. I've come back because I'm ill.' The tone was defiant.

'Where were you all this time? Where did you work?' Eva asked defensively; she did not want to hear.

'Bangkok, Hong Kong, Taiwan. Bars, massage parlours, cabarets. Need you ask? Japanese girls are always in demand. I made good money.' Kyo shrugged. There were fine lines about the corners of her eyes.

'And you never came back to Japan?' Eva questioned, feeling suddenly tired, suddenly old. There was a weight behind her lids.

'Sometimes, for visits.' Kyo shrugged again.

'But you didn't think then of Akiko?' Eva controlled the anger replacing the first harsh shock.

'She was all right. I knew you would look after her.' Kyo brazened.

'What makes the difference now?' Eva kept her voice low. She remembered how Kyo's well-being had obsessed her long before, and felt a double anger. What a fool I am, she thought.

Why did I let her in? She must not be allowed to destroy us.

'I've told you, I'm ill. I can't work. I've no money. I'm still Akiko's mother, you can't change that.' Kyo uncrossed her legs and sat forward in her chair.

'There is no one else to help me. I've no other relatives left as you well know, no one else I can go to. What is to become of me?' She puffed hard at the cigarette, the butt now a limp grey worm on her lip. Eva stared at the stagnant smoke above the woman's head.

'What happened to all your money?' Her heart beat in her head, the words sat stale and furred in her mouth. She wondered if the whole charade was not some figment of a nightmare. She blinked and touched the plait of hair about her head, but Kyo was still before her.

'I spent it. There is nothing left. Somebody has to help me. You were always so kind ... I thought ... I have never forgotten ...' Eva tried not to hear the desperation.

'Where else can I turn to but Akiko and you? Akiko is old enough to earn a living. She must help me. There is no one else. No one.' Kyo lowered her voice suddenly and said the words persuasively, playfully almost, except for their careful rounding. Slyness passed in her face like a shadow, her gaze nakedly prospecting in the dead hot air of the room.

Eva held her eyes and saw in them only darkness and arithmetic. The room became tight about her. The odour of perfume and hot dust thickened. She spoke quickly.

'I'll get you some coffee.' The words sounded light and ridiculous.

2

Her eyes would not adjust to the dim space after the sun-filled room. Eva felt her way blindly along the short passage until her fingers touched the kitchen door. She slid it open and the glass panes shook like teeth in old gums. Inside, she leaned against it, the wooden lattice about the glass pushed into her back. Before her the brown of wood and slopped meals stained the room; it contained this history in a dank ripe smell.

She placed two cups on a flowered lacquer tray. Soon the kettle belched hotly, frosting the window above. In the pan the simmering bones, thick with scum, covered her face with fusty steam. Replacing the lid she picked up the kettle; on the window condensation shrank from the corners of the glass. Behind the mist the ungainly facade of St. Christopher's orphanage could be seen. Eva had worked with the orphanage for many years. She had come to Japan when her father left England for a posting in Japan, and had finished her education in a mission school in Kobe. When she left, returning to England for medical studies, her parents stayed on in Japan. But soon after she qualified they were killed in a car crash, and she returned to settle their affairs just before the war broke out. Her work with the mission started when she returned to Japan with the Red Cross after the war had ended, during the American occupation. Soon, the orphanage had begun to take shape, a few nuns and herself, working from a derelict barracks with a handful of orphans and destitute women. It all grew from there, and afterwards she took the job the mission offered, happy to stay on. She never married.

Eva sighed, picked up the tray and walked back to the room, calmer. From outside she heard the creak of boards as Kyo moved around. As Eva opened the door, Kyo powdered her nose before the mirror. Sun burnished to a blatant copper her coarse and much-dyed hair that darkened at the roots. Her narrow back reflected all the awareness of a coquette. Eva placed the tray on the edge of the table. Within a cup her own face stared up at her, mirrored in the thin black liquid. She broke it quickly with a stream of milk.

At the beginning she had told the child, Akiko, I do not know. Pushing down the wish to lie, to say, your mother is dead, do not ask of her, it is I who am your mother. She stilled the wish and told the half-truth calmly. I do not know. But the child insisted. Where is she? Who is she? She must be somewhere still? My real mother. Even when she reached an age when she no longer asked, Eva knew she kept that childhood persistence locked in her still. Who is she? Where is she? Akiko would ask herself forever.

'I cannot persuade the child to accept you, one way or the other. It is for her to decide, not I. But I must tell you, she does not think as you do. She has not been brought up in a Japanese way. And you could not have expected that when you left her with me.' Stirring her coffee, Eva felt the grit of sugar scrape beneath her spoon.

'I suppose not.' Kyo shrugged indifferently. 'Is she here? Why don't you call her?'

'She's not here now. She's gone to work.' Eva spoke slowly. She pictured an innocent Akiko amongst tables of break-fasting orphans.

'What work?' Kyo looked up abruptly. 'Is she earning money already?' Her eyes took on new interest.

'She took a course in kindergarten teaching when she left

school. It was what she wanted to do. Now she works in the orphanage with me,' Eva replied.

'You could call her from there. It's only across the road.'

'No.' For she could face no more that day. The stagnant heat filled the room, and from the garden came the rasping saw of a cricket.

'No,' Eva repeated. 'Perhaps I should prepare her.' Though how she did not know.

'I'll go then.' Kyo stood up and stubbed out her cigarette in an ashtray. She coughed and the ash blew up in a fragile cloud and settled on a bowl of yellow daisies. She straightened, tiny and bony as a little bird. But her neck was arched, stringy and deliberate and her long thin eyes glittered, dark.

'There is no need to prepare her. I have written already, several days ago.' She turned before Eva out of the room. 'I'll be in touch now, you'll be hearing from me.'

Eva returned slowly to the lounge. Kyo. Akiko. She sat down again, and the last hour seemed like a dream. It was already only nine thirty. It was her own fault, she thought bitterly. She had allowed the years to pass in false certainty. The moon left a silver trail across the bay each night, and shone transparent in the morning. She had watched it each day, unfaltering, and saw the future sure and safe. She adopted the child legally, and it seemed as if Kyo was dead. Eva ceased to fear her presence, existing somewhere in the world. The child lived with her, safe and close. In the dark she could reach out and touch her. Nothing else mattered.

Now she remembered again the night she found Kyo, thrown into a Tokyo gutter, after the war. She was only eighteen, gashed and bruised and gaunt on subsistence food. She had broken the organised code of the streets and tried to run away. After the war, her farmer father had sold her into the red-light world, to provide for her brothers who were of use on the land. A heartbreaking but honourable course of action. Destitution was great at that time and from Tokyo they came round the villages in gangs, buying women and children. And Kyo was her parents' property. She obeyed a code of filial piety in Japan that decreed the debt incurred to parents at birth can never be repaid one ten thousandth in life. It was a sense of duty quite unknown in the West. And prostitution in Japan was not by tradition a dishonourable life. Throughout history Japanese women were divided by fate into either wives or harlots.

Eva had taken Kyo back to Kobe. The girl worked in the orphanage and Eva taught her English. She became bright and plump and laughed. When it seemed right Eva found her a job as a maid in the family of an American commander on a military base at Iwakuni. There was the prospect of her returning with the family to America. But Kyo soon left her job, and Eva never knew why, for Kyo chose to cut all ties. Later Eva heard she was working in a bar on the outskirts of the camp, well paid for the English she spoke now, but back in her old profession.

The room still held Kyo's perfume captive, a luminous, fleshy smell that lingered. Beneath Eva's closed lids, Kyo floated before her still. In her face the lips were a provocative purple flower, secretive and unyielding. Words came back to Eva one by one, hard and shiny as chips of glass. 'I have written already, several days ago.' The words repeated in her mind.

Now, in the chair, Eva felt her body too unwieldy a thing to move. In the garden the glowering heat and dry grey soil dissolved beneath the marigolds that bloomed in a scorched and garish eruption of colour. Time stretched before her like polished metal upon which she slipped. Through the window, in spite of the heat, she noticed a dense bank of cloud in the sky, silent and unmoving. Outside in a tree sparrows quarrelled, their throats deft and sweet and hard. Around her were doors she could not shut. And she saw it then across the room: Kyo's empty coffee cup. On its rim a purple lip stained the sun-filled room. There was a drumming in her head.

3

In a room above where Eva Kraig sat, her nephew Daniel lay down again, fully dressed upon the bed, and closed his eyes. His head ached. Soon he would have to begin the day, soon he would have to go down. He could not put it off; he must show a visitor's politeness. In the room it was hot. When he first arrived, they had excused him, allowed him to shut himself away up here, to get over the journey from New York; it had not been so bad, he had slept on the plane. But he used the excuse to disappear, hide. He had no wish to see them. He had no wish to be here. But his mother had insisted.

'It will be good for you, Daniel, just what you need to get over that terrible accident.' So he had arranged a holiday from the law firm in which he was a junior partner. And come here to Japan. But he doubted he would ever get over the accident. He had been here now two weeks.

Above him the ceiling was unpolished wooden boards, he followed the graining with his eyes, playing with the patterns. He came back to the single image of a hand poised above him, and turned on his side to escape it. He had not slept well, waking several times to the smell of night flowers in Eva's garden. Looking from the window, he had seen in the porch light the small cerise trumpets open and bright. While everything slept their scent filled the dark garden like something living, sensual and thick. And mixed, as he feared, with his dreams when he slept, becoming the smell of damp grass when he came to after the accident. Since it he had been dreaming a lot, bad dreams. He had not told anyone, he did not want more fuss.

The room was small and fragile; it shook as he walked around, so that he felt it might collapse upon him like a house of cards. He had to bend his head to enter the door. He felt unbearably confined, in a box, heat stifled in the smallness of it all. He sat down and twiddled the knobs of a radio on a shelf, listening absently to the crackle of stations and the bright piping of unintelligible language. He heard the sudden comfort of a Southern drawl and turned the needle back, to the Far East Forces network, and listened to the news, half-heartedly.

They had been waiting for him at the airport. He had not seen Eva since he was ten. But she seemed as he remembered. The same firm expression and clear blue eyes above her half moon glasses. The flesh of her face was white and still, like the flesh of meditative nuns. Her hair was plaited as he remembered, but grey now, wound tightly round her head, archaic and absurd as her glasses. Yet she possessed a strange elegance, and she held herself very upright. Beside her was the girl, Akiko, whom he had seen only in photographs. Her father had been an American serviceman, he could see the occidental in her. Something struggled from the small cast of oriental bones, something that followed the form but lifted free. And she was nearly as tall as Eva, long-legged, not a Japanese body. She twitched nervously at the strap of her bag. She was not what he expected; she was beautiful.

He lay down again upon the bed.

'In Los Angeles last night a man attempted to hijack an airliner with a toy pistol. The airliner was ...' The radio droned on.

In the room the sultry air weighed upon him, the sweep of a standing fan did not break the humidity. He closed his eyes. These days he was always tired, he awoke as if he had not slept. Through the window the sun pressed orange whorls upon his lids, dilating and spinning. He put a hand protec-tively across his eyes and turned his head away. And the world was suddenly dark and green. Like when he had come to in the car with Casey at the time of the accident, deep beneath the water. It was like a dream now, a dark sealed vault at the back of his mind that kept opening. He remembered again the car's fall from the low wooden bridge, like a film that went very slowly. It seemed to fall forever. Then the impact as it hit the river, and the blackness. He came to in a murky aqueous world, and remembered bubbles released from his mouth, perfect and round. Casey's head was slumped in Daniel's lap. From it hair flowed up on end, like delicate weeds, waving gently in the motion of the water. He had thought in terror, he is dead, and frantically pulled at Casey's body. But he was heavy and slack and would not move. He tried to open the car door to drag Casey out, but the weight of the water held it closed. His head began to spin, his lungs burst in pain, and he had manoeuvred himself out and up through the open window, desperate for air, leaving Casey.

I'll dive down again, I'll bring him out, he thought, swimming upwards.

Light blazed as he hit the surface. Then he remembered nothing until he came to again in the warm grass of the river bank, the sun hot on his sodden clothes. He watched an ant walk the length of a stalk, and heard voices on the bridge. And immediately it came back to him then. He knew the bridge well, he and Casey often came here at weekends, to fish. He should have known better, should have gone more carefully over the bridge. But they were laughing stupidly, so that he had not seen the child at first, wobbling precariously towards them on a bicycle much too big for her. She could not have been more than nine. He pulled the car to the left too late, and that too was slow in his mind, the graceful loop her body turned in the air. Then the thud as she hit the windshield, and was flung into the water.

There were people on the bridge. Sitting in the grass he had watched them absently, unable to associate himself with the scene. He saw them pull the child's body from the water, then the bike. Sun glinted on the wet spokes of wheels, he heard their vacant spinning. It was all very distant, nothing to do with him.

But he remembered Casey suddenly then, and thought, I did nothing. I did not go back, I lost consciousness. I did not save him. I thought only of myself. He saw they had noticed him then from the bridge. They came towards him, holding out their hands, faces filled with relief and concern. I could not save him, he thought again. Nothing else filled his mind.

Now he shook his head on the pillow, trying physically to rid himself of the memories. He sat up and tried to listen to the radio. The voice came to him, a comforting twang, and pulled him back into the present.

Standing, his mind and body felt heavy. In the window the

mosquito netting was clogged with dust. Behind it he saw in the distance the brimming, passive sea, the oily surface of its skin reflecting clouds. Switching off the radio he stretched his arms above his head and prepared to face the day. He would have to go down now. He must not disappoint them, they were doing so much for him. He thought of the girl Akiko again, and walked towards the door.

4

Up the hill from Eva Kraig's, in a one-storeyed house with a patch of lawn and two topiary bushes of holly and privet, the Englishman, Arthur John Wilcox, worked at his map. Kobe in 1870. Red ink for the native town, blue for the foreign bits. My Work, he said. My Work. And planned to withdraw from flippant society. He even looked askance at Eva Kraig, met on an evening walk, who asked after his recent retirement.

'Retirement, Doctor, is a living death. It is not for me, oh no, to sit around the bar at the club, waiting for the company of any Tom, Dick or Harry with whom to sip a drink, to pass away the day. We must make use of each phase of life. I have within me still, I am thankful to say, a mine of untapped resources. I have taken up History, Doctor. Taken up History.' He walked off, back straight as a ramrod, stroking his moustache in a preoccupied way. For the idea was growing within him since the day before, since the visit of Geraldine Cooper. Plump and smart and tightly corseted, she had sat before him in his home and changed his ebbing life, an answer to his prayer. For after six months of premature retirement the future gaped, contemptuous. And still filled him with fury. For what right had they had to pension him off so much earlier than they needed to.

'Young men, young blood. Only way to survive,' said the new forty-two year old chairman of Murdoch and Hack. 'And corporations. No room for the small firm today.' Within a year there had been the merger with an American conglomerate.

'Our new policy demands ...' began the young man, and the committee behind him nodded. Within ten minutes they disposed of Arthur and the service of forty years. They gave him a watch on a bed of red satin in a small black plastic box. He went home in a daze.

'But I am young.' He roared the words at a freckle-faced mirror, and punched his muscular chest. 'Not many half my age as fit as I. Still in the club tennis team, winner of the annual golf cup eight times. Not a twinge of arthritis, not a day's indigestion. Young whippersnappers, set themselves up as God nowadays. They'll learn, soon come crawling for advice.' He straightened his tie in the mirror, smoothed back a head of thick grey hair and remarked at the healthy glow of his skin, stretched firmly on his bones. No droop or drag there, ten minutes of facial exercises a day accomplished that for him. For comfort he stroked the corpulence of a rather flamboyant moustache. Loath to give in entirely to age, it still contained a few ginger hairs. And he remembered with satisfaction that his recent ex-employer was bald at forty-two. 'Bah.' He spat out at the empty room.

The day, in spite of a plentiful curriculum of sports and activity, could not contain the void of work. It allowed him time to think, which was always a bad thing. All evils occurred from too much thought. An involved and active mind, exhausted in

constructive work, had no energy at the end of the day to roam
the more dubious byways. Such was the experience of Arthur
Wilcox. But retirement presented a breach of this contract
with his mind. Widening cracks appeared in the dikes, through
which trepidations leaked. He was terrified by thoughts of
his old friend, Spencer, who had died the week before. Since
then the morbid fear of death hung over him all the time, an
ache that subsided only to start again. Spencer. He pushed the
thought from him. Geraldine Cooper would change all that.
She offered purpose to his life.

'I am hesitant, Mr Wilcox, to disturb your tranquil retirement, but the committee was unanimous. We have chosen
you, yes, we have decided. Nobody else has all the requirements,
the knowledge and experience. It is for the centenary of the club,
and as you know a history of the club will be nearly a history
of the foreign community in Kobe. It should be a substantial
pamphlet, Mr Wilcox. The committee has gathered a collection
of old photographs which we also wish to include. It will be
most exciting. Now do say you will do it?'

Geraldine Cooper smiled from her chair, a confident,
authoritative smile. She touched her hair and smoothed her
skirt across her knees. Filling the space between them Arthur
was aware of a flowery perfume, and could not remember
when a woman was last in the room. Once in a while Eva
Kraig visited, with a bag of fruit and a magazine, and some
part of each day the old woman, Onishi-san, came in to clean.
But he did not think them feminine forms comparable with
Geraldine Cooper. There was no frivolity about Eva Kraig,
with her half-moon glasses. Onishi-san was gold toothed and
sixty-nine. But he had to admit Geraldine Cooper was no

longer the fresh-cheeked girl he had met, not long after he came to Kobe.

The English were a large community then, and stuck together. Arthur played billiards with Horace Bingham, Geraldine's father, each Wednesday in the club, and often attended the musical evenings Horace and his wife, Maud, arranged at their home. Horace played the violin, Maud the piano, Arthur accompanied on the flute. Geraldine, in bows and lace-edged pinafore ran, maid in tow, about the room. But Horace died early, Maud was now senile and Geraldine had rashly married an American who arrived in Kobe and insinuated his way into Horace's business. Once, after a gin, Maud had privately confided her doubts to Arthur about Anglo-American marriages. 'It is an adolescent country, Arthur, no history, no culture, what will they have in common?' She placed a hand on his arm, tears in her eyes. After the marriage and Horace's death, Nate Cooper made money hand over fist. There was now nobody richer in Kobe. But for Arthur the friendship ended with Horace's death; he had little in common with young Nate Cooper.

In spite of its pleasantness Geraldine's perfume set up an allergy in his nose and his eyes began to prick. Each time she moved a faint rustle sounded. Against all contrary effort, his mind wandered as to what underclothing might cause that gentle rub, and was ashamed, for it was unlike him; he was not that sort of man. But these were the wilful ways of his mind, idle in retirement. Geraldine's perfume had its way. Arthur sneezed ungraciously, spraying spittle upon his moustache.

'A cup of tea? Well then, a cold drink?' he suggested, to prolong the encounter, to put off the emptiness that stretched beyond.

Mixing a cordial in the kitchen, the strange feminine presence of Geraldine Cooper seeped through the walls. In the glass on the tray, ice bobbed up and down in a raspberry sea, and clunked on the tall thin sides. A mosquito whined near his ear, its previous attack itched on his wrist. He swished a dish cloth discouragingly about, impatient. For he was suddenly filled with suppressed excitement, a restlessness such as he felt after a couple of whiskeys.

Handing Geraldine the cordial he watched her fingertips leave warm patches on the frosty glass. As she took a sip ice bumped her mouth. She looked up and smiled approvingly. Standing before her, staring down, he noted the solid packing of her flesh, noted she must be fifty now, and that brown pencil made the hard line of her brows. But at the drape of her neckline the flesh swam briefly, free and white, soft as clotted cream, before being coffined in its corset. He could not draw his eyes away and prayed for Geraldine Cooper both to go and to stay from the safety of his chair.

But after she left he was no longer alone. The idea was wedged in him firmly. He would write the pamphlet about the club, and then a history of the foreign community in Kobe. The idea grew in his mind, devouring the bareness before him. He began at once to search out old books. In the morning, he started the map.

He had the little ink bottles in a row before him now, the blue, the red, black for lettering, green for hills and rural land. There was a lot of green then, in the old days, when the first foreigners settled in Kobe. He shaded in the hump of two hills, and the thought of old Spencer was with him again, constricting his throat and mind. On the desk the bottles of ink caught the sun and showed secret jewelled interiors, blue as summer dusk, red as blood. Red as blood. Like the bottles that had hung over Spencer in the hospital, just a week and a day ago. But the blood had not helped Spencer. Spencer had died. Spencer was dead.

Arthur John Wilcox mixed green ink with a drop of black in a saucer to his right, to hatch in match-stick pines, to darken the Kobe hills. And tried not to think of Spencer who had died alone in a bland white room, beneath tubes and bottles of blood. Not even a nurse in sight.

'Won't come.' Spencer had croaked, his lips scaly, his skin the colour of sour porridge. 'Not like the old days. Not a good morning or how are you today. A chewed up lot. Now you press this here bell and they speak to you through that contraption in the ceiling.' The words rattled hoarsely in Spencer's throat, his eyes gestured blearily before they closed, and he lay too exhausted to speak.

During the week since Spencer's death the world had closed in about Arthur's soul. He had taken it badly, he knew. The greater thoughts to life, frightful in their bareness, baited him with reality now. He muttered the words under his breath. All must die. All must go. All are born to that end. And felt even worse.

Kobe Foreign Settlement or Concession, Arthur printed neatly across an area of blue squares. Native town, he wrote across a similar area in red. Ikuta Shrine. Ono Foreign Cemetery. Then, on a separate piece of paper he tried a few simplified drawings of sailing ships and junks that might afterwards be settled in the bay and harbour.

He did not want to die like Spencer, alone. It was as much the aloneness as the death that took him by the throat now. For, one by one, he had seen them go, all the old timers, as the foreign community now called those such as Arthur. Their deaths he had accepted, never equating the state with himself. Old age seemed always a distance away; he had not been ready to enter the phase. But here he was, six months retired and already that cast-off feeling a heavy pit in his stomach, depression slowing him down.

In the garden, beyond the windows, the stiff bulbous shadow of a topiaried bush was spread upon the lawn, in the distance the bay opened out under great banks of cloud. Arthur looked at the bush and then at the cloud and found a topiary likeness. Beneath the sky the sea was the colour of bile. 'Bad weather near,' muttered Arthur, and bent his head to his desk. Carefully he began copying from a book. 'An old diagrammatic map of Hiogo Port, later known as Kobe Port, during the opening years of the Foreign Settlement or Concession around 1870, before the Ikuta river was diverted to the Shin Ikuta River in 1871 and before the railway from Osaka was opened in 1874.'

At the funeral there had been only himself and Father Richards from the Catholic Church. A representative from the International Committee of Kobe had failed to arrive and phoned later to apologise, with an excuse. It was a young man's voice, American. He confessed at Arthur's inquiry that he had not known Spencer, only visited him once, in the hospital. But, he explained, the committee was a charitable organisation of the international community, exactly for purposes of aid to destitute old foreigners like Spencer.

'He was not destitute, not destitute at all, sir, I'll have you know,' Arthur roared down the phone. 'Only old and lonely, which I suppose to a youngster like you appears a sin of charitable proportions.' There was a lump in his throat on behalf of Spencer.

'I mean destitute in the spiritual sense.' The young man quickly said. 'You know, shipwrecked upon his own island. No sense of belonging, no home to go home to, living in limbo. Just lived here too long, I suppose.'

The tone of voice was light. Arthur detected a note of derision. Arthur had put down the phone, and his fingers shook. For Spencer had been destitute. Although he refused to admit it, living alone with his dog in the evil-smelling wooden house he had been reduced to. Once a week Arthur had climbed the rickety outside staircase to Spencer's rooms on the second floor, and ducked beneath the dripping underwear, an eternal hazard there. The dog was stout and stiff like Spencer, with more, Arthur suspected, than a touch of the mange. The place smelled of animal, stale blankets and hard, old-fashioned shaving soap. Spencer wore shoes without any laces, his shirt was stained with food. It was shocking the way he had let himself go. And Arthur felt responsible, could not bear to see the dreadful fall in circumstance; for Spencer had once been his boss, when Arthur first arrived in Japan to join the old British trading firm of Murdoch and Hack. Then Spencer had been a dapper man of quick neat movements and small plump hands, dimpled like a woman's. Arthur respected his low voice of command, his way with the ladies, his presidency of the club, that unparalleled authority in the foreign community. But times changed, war came, Spencer grew older, married at fifty a Japanese woman, separated, retired, grew sick, was divested one way or another of all he had, and never returned to England. Old friends died one by one, younger people filled the foreign community, and did not know of Spencer. Arthur had stayed with Murdoch and Hack after Spencer left in search of better things, but for Spencer it had only been downhill. Arthur brooded over the change in things, behind his paper in the club, which now allowed women and even tolerated children and open-necked shirts in the bar. They were all young people here now with international companies, who came to Japan on short contracts. In the old days if you chose to venture this far you stayed, usually a lifetime.

Under the heading Notes, Arthur began to write. 'New Year's Day, 1868, was the appointed day for the opening of Kobe, or Hiogo as it was then called, to foreign trade ...' A mosquito whined again about his ear. He swished it off and saw it settle on the folded square of the newspaper on the desk. Its delicate insolence disturbed the grey meeting of two politicians in a mottled photograph. Arthur took aim with a thick envelope and the insect became a bloody mark. But the quick movement caught a small blue vase on a corner of the desk. It crashed to the floor and broke; he stared down at the fragments in dismay. The vase had stood on his desk for twenty years. Sometimes he stuck a flower in it. Sometimes. He picked up the bits and looked at them in the palm of his hand, at the smooth film of blue glaze on the shattered earthenware. He turned them over in his hand, and remembered the woman, Kyo, again.

5

She had no need to read the letter; she knew the words by heart. They echoed and gnawed in Akiko's head. And sometimes they sang, scarlet and flowered. Even the neat, flexed columns of Japanese characters, arriving from their indeterminate source, were not strange. Because of the familiarity of the emotion they aroused. She had suspected nothing when she picked up the letter, although she had dreamed of it often. And afterwards she told nobody. Not even Eva.

The sun was already hot on her face, although it was early. But today in a sultry way; unnatural. She had not slept well, the letter cutting her adrift from rest, so that she had seen the dawn, and a strange sickly cast to the sky that filled her with unease. Akiko, the letter started. Akiko, you will not know me and yet sometimes I like to hope you think of me. And afterwards she had answered, I do. Often. And she had said the word aloud: Mother. It had a strange thick feel in her mouth, stiff as unused rubber. She had not tried again. That was two days ago. Since then she carried the letter inside her, a whole fantastic landscape before which she trembled, poised, afraid that at darkness or a touch it would soundlessly disappear. But at such times she stared again at the letter, taking it from a small lacquer box. Unfolding it carefully, her hands trembled and anticipated an identity to be restored. On the page, the ink of the biro still secreted an oily glaze. Like leggy insects, the delicate fragments of each character lay hatched in neat columns. They joined to make sentences, palpable and whole that quickened in her throat.

Akiko, sometimes I like to hope you think of me.

Mother. Mother.

She handled the letter wonderingly, like precious glass, and could not speak in case it broke. But inside she waited, intuitively, knowing this was the beginning. She did not answer; she knew there was no need.

In the yard of the orphanage she sat beneath the wisteria, legs stretched out to the sun. The leaves were beginning to yellow, the frenzied mass of branches trapped heat and the crackle of insects. She looked up into its complicated darkness, warmth beat down upon her. She thought again of Daniel, and somehow they seemed tied up together, man and letter, setting the world upon its end.

From the dining room door two children ran out. In the yard they began to bounce a purple ball. On the chest of their T-shirts gaudy pictures jumped and jerked. Akiko pulled herself up, calling them behind her for breakfast. They were all trooping in now, filling the room like a tide. She counted heads as they darted and pushed. Mariko ... Yumiko ... Takeo ... Jun ... Some little ones passed her in a file, a clump of four joined hands to waists, hopping and chanting. The sun speared windows and fell in a path of lozenges on the linoleum floor. The children hopped from one bright pool to the next, singing.

At one time Hanako's
Tears poured down
Poured down,
Too many tears
Too many tears,
With a kimono sleeve
Let us wipe the tears ...

She remembered the old song and watched breath vibrating in the small bodies as the thick polished helmets of the girls' hair flapped up and down. Emiko's plaits rapped her shoulders, fringes were disturbed and parted. Watching, Akiko saw herself again, walking to the same tables, long before.

She straightened chairs behind small backs, tied Emiko's

bib, parted the battling chopsticks of Takeo, Nobuo and Jun. They settled and the pink stain of ginger pickles soon became part of Nobuo's shirt. Behind, the older children ate in a more subdued manner. Mariko and Yumiko sat together in an uneasy truce, after an argumentative week. Beside them Hiroshi's fingers stuck out like fat grubs from the plaster of his broken arm. Soon they only simmered beneath the clatter of chopsticks and bowls, and the lusty suck of soup. These sounds, this room, had been with her always. Although she had lived with Eva, during the day there were no differences made. So that now the room settled comfortably around her. At the tables were the bent heads of children, the small bowls of rice, the magenta of pickles, the smooth nests of eggs. The same breakfast hour she had known throughout her life; she felt safe and grateful for it. She bent and broke a raw egg into Hiroshi's bowl.

'Jiro is still outside.' He pointed with his chopsticks to the yard. 'He's talking to the flowers again.' Hiroshi guffawed and sprayed soup upon the table.

Akiko saw then Jiro was missing, his seat empty at the table. They called him Jiro, although on his records there was a Korean name. But it was better, said Eva, that he took the protective hide of a Japanese name, for his mother was Japanese, even if his father was Korean; he would not show up like a naked thing on a printed register. In that way he might for a while postpone the hate he must receive in Japan for the double sin of being of mixed blood and also Korean.

Akiko found him in the garden. He was under the camellia tree that in spite of the heat had burst its first flower, an awkward early bloom. He was a strange and introverted child. In the thick of other children's conversations, he rarely spoke; he looked out at the world in a guarded way, as if protecting something too delicate to expose. And he drew, absorbed constructions that he said were magic flowers or complicated underworlds. As she walked towards him he picked the solitary bloom and held it to his face. He was the oldest child in the orphanage.

'Don't you want your breakfast?' she asked.

'They say you must never bring these into the house. Camellia don't drop petal by petal, they fall like severed heads. Is that true? Is it unlucky?' He turned thoughtful eyes upon her, waiting.

'Not much you are told like that is true. You must decide these things for yourself. It is only what you decide that is important.' She told him because she remembered long before, standing beneath the same camellia, before the dusty body of a dead bird: a neatly folded brown and beige soul, except for the maggots that crawled in its eyes. And that treachery had somehow seemed the shape of life.

He paused to consider. 'Then I shall take it inside.'

Akiko nodded, she knew him. Inwardly he was like her, divided, dissolved, yet of one hard shape. He must search the arrangements of other people for the clues that were himself. She walked back behind him into the room.

With his arm in a plaster cast, Hiroshi held his chopsticks awk-wardly, beating a raw egg in his bowl. It slipped and spilt an oily yellow mess over his legs. Akiko reached for a bowl and cloth and sponged his fat brown knees. Fat square knees like the boy Daniel in the photograph Eva kept of him upon her dressing table. An old photograph, taken when Daniel was four. Now he must be thirty. This morning Eva had told her to take Daniel to the festival at the local shrine. The thought of being alone with him knocked inside her head.

Until now there had been just that photo of Daniel. A photo she had stared at secretly in childhood, trying to resurrect. And she had always thought, some part of Eva flows within him that does not flow in me. In his face she detected the similar outline of an ear, the eye laid firm and forthright in a way that was familiar. He is hers, she thought, not me. She looked at him curiously, looking beyond Eva for that link within him that was her father. A link as wide as a continent, and as narrow as the word, America. That was all she knew of her father; the word, American. Yet, through her childhood she had tried to find him, painfully, rashly, in mottled newsprint photographs, improbable music and atlas names. She searched in darkness among those American families she met through Eva, but found no comforting revelation. Only a dry discarded dust, and loneliness in her veins.

She had asked Eva many times when small, lying in bed, staring up from the pillow into her face. 'Who are they? Where are they? My parents?' She looked up into the woman's face; a broad, firm, loving face. But she saw only the look that came into the eyes, the shadow that closed the face.

'Do not think backwards. I am here instead to love you. Your mother left you with me, to love, she wanted it that way. And where she is now, I do not know. Your father was American. Of him I know nothing more than that. She never told me.'

'What did she look like?'

'Pretty.'

'How pretty?'

'Very.'

The child saw then the lips were shut, and held a finished

look that would release no more. If Eva knew, it was concealed, in some dark compartment, unpronounceable, however much the child's heart ticked beneath the serge of school uniform. Akiko had ceased to ask the useless questions. She managed to hold them in silent, so that they lay close to her bones.

Sometimes, as a child, she had been invited to play at the homes of Eva's foreign friends. She had gone eagerly at first. In the houses of missionaries and consuls she played with blue-eyed children who played with blue-eyed dolls. And her head began to spin, on the very edge of it all. Here she could reach out and touch her father's world, but however hard she tried she could hold none of it in her hand. The sharp features and flaccid skins, the coca-colas and peanut butter, and soft slurred vowels of women with floury baking hands, the men with bony eyes, pink iced birthday cakes, petit point cushions, the bulge of toes in a pair of old shoes, a cat asleep beneath bed covers. As a world it rose up and rejected her.

'Here, in your own country, you may be considered beautiful, but not in America,' a violet-eyed child once told her, plaiting flaxen braids before a mirror.

'My father is American.'

'You don't say?' retorted the child. 'Where is he then? Where is he?'

The hungriness in Akiko retreated, rolling back upon itself. She went less and less.

'But it's good for you. Why must you be so difficult? Well, do as you wish,' sighed Eva, having always a maze of other children to consume her.

Sometimes Eva sent her along the road to Mrs Okuno's, to play with the daughters there.

'Your nose, your nose,' they screamed. 'It looks like a *Bugaku* mask.'

And Mrs Okuno's senile mother would sit on winter days beside a heavy wooden brazier, grilling sticky *mochi* rice cakes upon a wire mesh. She brushed them with soya until they gleamed caramel and the sauce dripped and spat on the coals beneath.

'Little *konketsu*, mixed-blood one, come here.' She laid a bony, long-clawed hand upon the child, a hand already dead. Her eyes were like ferrets', buried deep down. 'You should not have been born. There is no place for you here. Your mother should have killed herself with shame. But not her. I knew her. She would lay with them in the open if they paid her enough. She left you in a box on that English-woman's doorstep. Yes, your own mother didn't want you, you shameful thing.' She cackled, her face ripped open by grey mottled teeth. She held a hot, skewered rice cake up to Akiko's face. Once, she pressed it to the child's lips; there had been a blister for a week.

It was almost the same in the Japanese school they went to from the orphanage. Then, there had been others like herself in the orphanage, a forgotten population, after the war and the occupation. '*Konketsu*', mixed blood, they called after the orphanage crocodile in the street. Voices stopped suddenly when Akiko appeared; the desk beside her had been vacant half a year.

Akiko had preferred the orphanage, where there were others like herself. It offered some bleak unity; the unity of a group of wanderers on the spine of a hill at sunset. But she grew there in peace, undisturbed. She sensed the silence within each child, whittled and thin as bone. It drew them together in a soundless way, beneath the clatter of lunchtime bowls, or the splash of the communal bath. Each battled alone, discarded by the world.

Before the breakfasting children now, Akiko remembered the letter again. The thought swelled in her. I'm not like them, I'm different now. For it seemed like that. It seemed the letter made her different.

Mother. She whispered it soundlessly again.

6

In the Coopers' house at the bottom of the hill, old Maud Bingham lay in bed and called for her daughter, Geraldine.

'Geraldine. Geraldine. Oh why do you not come?' The breakfast tray was heavy on her knees and behind her the pillows had slipped and bunched awkwardly, leaving her neck unsupported. There was egg yolk on her nightdress. Things had never been the same since they moved to this house.

'Horace,' she said, for she thought she saw her husband standing there beside the bed, the sun reflected on the chain of his pocket watch. 'Horace. Tell Geraldine to take this tray away.'

But there was only silence to answer Maud Bingham and the rustle of a curtain in the sliver of a breeze. She opened her eyes then. Horace was not there. It was only the gleam of a metal photo frame. Nothing more. She must remember to remember Horace was dead. But it was increasingly difficult to secure these minor details in her mind. For the moment she shut her eyes he was there again, strutting impatiently up and down.

'Maud. Maud,' he called. She was sure she heard him say it.

There were times like this every day now, when the thin rim

between dreams and realities dissolved and the two mixed. And she did not mind but waited for it, for the memories reassured, like the touch of hands, like the faded smiles of photographs and the yellow faces of old letters. She shut her eyes and let the past reclaim her.

And there were Mama and Papa again. Mama in a blue bustled autumn dress with the engraved silver clasps of two storks beneath a cherry tree. Maud was in pink with rosebuds on her boater. A *jinriksha* waited for them at the door. They were to go to the fireworks at Ryogoku Bridge. They had gone to a tea house, called The House of a Thousand Mats, and were offered seats in the gardens there where a fine view of the river and fireworks was obtained. The river was alive with the lanterns of lighted gondolas carrying *geisha* and their patrons. The clipped notes of the *samisen* filled the air. The fireworks were the best she had ever seen.

She had been only six when she came to Japan with her parents, when her father was invited to fill a post at Tokyo University. She never left. Horace came out at twenty-two with the London and Lancashire Insurance Company. They had met at a croquet match at a Mrs de Boinville's.

'Geraldine. Geraldine,' she cried in vain.

The window was open, a huge steel-framed hole. She could see the bay, still and flat beneath fleshy clouds, near enough to touch, it seemed. It frightened her, this crag hanging over the sea that Nate Cooper, her son-in-law, insisted upon. She preferred the old house, high on the hill, but she of course was voiceless, an old woman in need of a home. Her son-in-law had many times doubled Horace's business; it was not for her to complain. But she longed for the familiarity of the old home she had come to with Horace. He had died there, Geraldine grew up there. But Nate did not care. She should have heeded her instincts and all she had heard about the brashness of Americans. But Geraldine had been getting on, there were few opportunities for a girl of her age in Japan, few eligible foreign men. No, Nate did not care. He brought in the wreckers and replaced the house with obnoxious flats. And moved them down here, into this concrete fortress, hugging the bay. She did not recall how long they had been here, one year or ten. The days slipped in and out of her mind until they were as one. But you could not knock a nail into the wall, she remembered that clearly. To hang up her mother's old prints of the Lake District and Horace's collection of early Meiji woodblock prints, that were all so dear to her, a man with an electric drill was called in. She had lain in bed and watched him with tears in her eyes. The drill screamed in her ears, the concrete dust could be tasted on the tongue. It had all worn her out.

'I want to go home,' she had cried.

'Don't be silly, Mother. This is home. That rickety old place was most unsafe and no longer practical. No, Nate has quite surpassed himself with this. Now, is there anyone you would like to add to the housewarming guests?' But of course there was not, and her daughter knew it. All Maud's contemporaries were dead.

From the shore she heard the sound of waves, endlessly folding and unfolding. Around her flat walls stared down, on her lap the heavy tray held her captive. She saw her own hand then on the sheet and did not recognise it at first: a sinewy brown stained stick. Was this her hand? It bore no resemblance to the hands she remembered. I am old, she thought suddenly. For she recalled a birthday cake some time before, she remembered pink iced numbers upon it. She moved back in the bed in fear. I am old, she thought again, and the words splintered into light.

She tried to sit up but her body was heavy and would not obey. Slowly she drew her legs up, and the tray slipped from her lap. The crash cut about in her head. She dared not open her eyes or look, just lay waiting, imagining the mass of half boiled yolk and eggshell on the carpet.

'Geraldine.' Nobody came.

7

Before her mirror in the bedroom Geraldine Cooper frowned, and listened to her mother call.

'Geraldine.'

She must wait. She must *learn* to wait, Geraldine Cooper said to herself. For I have many things in my life, responsibilities, a home to run. Many people are dependent upon me, upon my abilities. She thought of Eva Kraig's orphanage, the hospital, all the committees. I cannot sacrifice my life upon my mother's altar. I must keep my priorities straight. If things get too bad, we will employ a nurse, and maybe another maid.

'If things get too bad, Nate, we must employ a nurse.' She tilted the long oval mirror on its stand before her, and looked critically at the judgment thrown up. Behind her reflection Nate Cooper appeared to the side of the mirror, sitting slackly in a chair. He crossed an ankle on a knee and began to tie his laces, the blood strained in his face. Geraldine's eyes hardened. 'I said, if things get too bad, Nate, we must employ a nurse.'

'Sure, Honey, okay,' muttered Nate, still struggling with his shoes. Light from the window behind glistened on grooves of hair criss-crossing his balding skull. The sight filled Geraldine with repulsion. She turned her eyes away.

'Yes. A nurse would be just the thing. Or perhaps a companion with some nursing experience. I shall inquire, I shall go into the matter. For sooner or later there will be a need. I see it coming.' She stared at herself in the mirror, turning her plump profile this way and that.

'There will be the necessity of some retrimming on this, some new lace about the neck.' The dress smelled of time, of mothballs and rain, of candles and pianos. My grandmother's dress, a hundred years old, she would tell them all proudly. A real centenary dress for the centenary of the club.

While cleaning the attic of the old house before they moved away, she had found the dress in a mould-stained trunk. And knew at once, even though it had been several years before, she would wear it on that day. For she had begun to plan the centenary even then, planned it really for the dress. She had not, if she was honest, thought of the centenary until then. But she did not tell the club committee; nobody knew of the dress. It would be a surprise. And the committee had been unanimous in electing her to plan it all. 'Nobody else has your touch, Geraldine. Just look what you did for the Tennis Tournament Ball. Who else could have thought of all that?'

'I have not been to a school for club functions. I just use my imagination, that's all. I think somebody else should have a chance,' Geraldine had replied and she knew they would not agree.

She had repacked the dress carefully and sent it down here,

to their new house. A little out here, a little out there, and it would fit. She held her breath, straining in the tight dress. Released in the mirror the red velvet gown palpitated about her body and pushed up above it, supported on whale bones, the substance that was Geraldine. It spilt out, thick and smooth as arum, an eiderdown of flesh. In her fifties, she had recently and comfortingly read, a woman could still be attractive, in the mature yeasty way no young girl had. I shall go on a diet, thought Geraldine Cooper. I shall eat grapefruit and yoghurt and nothing else. For at least a whole week, or maybe five days.

In the mirror Nate Cooper was slouched in the chair, writing on an envelope, columns of calculations. In the mirror she saw the scratched pattern of figures. Nate's fingers bunched tightly round his pen. He blew cigarette smoke from his nose and ignored her. His eyes were inward looking things, and already at eight-thirty in the morning. Geraldine speared him a look, pursing her small mouth and whirling to face him. The heavy dress swished pleasantly about her ankles.

'Business, business, nothing but business. It's too early yet for work. I'll not have it. And your coffee is cold.' She pointed to the chalky skin on a brimming cup. 'You are well into the coronary years, Nate, you must learn to relax, get away from your work.' She would not, she decided, be intimidated. She would not be the one to ruin the day, so early in the morning. She tried the usual bright Geraldine.

He did not move his head, just raised his eyes to look at her above the frames of his spectacles. He waited for her to speak again.

'Now, I want an opinion from you on this dress. Take a good look now, dear. It was my grandmother's dress. One hundred years old. I shall wear it for the centenary of the club. Now, isn't it marvellous. What do you say?'

'Who do you think you are, Scarlett O'Hara?' He dropped his eyes to his figures again.

'Why must you always be so mean? Horrid man.' She stared at him bitterly and said no more. I hate you, she thought. I hate you. And wished for a way to tell him so. I should have left, she thought, many years ago. And could not think why she had not. But she would not allow him to destroy her, to depress her, to make her feel less than what she was, an attractive woman. And she had certain proof she was still that. Only yesterday Arthur Wilcox had looked at her continuously in an overt-eyed way. A look she did not care to analyse, but could not deny. He had not been able to disregard her neckline or her knees. She had been most embarrassed, she had been glad to leave. But afterwards, in the safety of her home, she had felt light-headed, like a young girl again.

Peace. God give me peace, Nate Cooper said silently. His wife was an ageing piece of fruit upon which the skin had begun to crease. She was an old queen from New Orleans. Could she not see the farce of herself in that ancient, ridiculous dress? And he would be made to accompany it to the centenary ball, dressed no doubt as a gay hussar. The prospect made him stand up quickly.

The air conditioning trampled heat in the room. Above the faint hum of the machine, Geraldine prepared to speak. 'The committee has decided they must set the example. All committee members and their partners will come in centenary dress, something of the period. It will create just the atmosphere we need. Everyone will be dressed like this, it will not be just me. It was not my idea. It was a unanimous decision.'

Nate Cooper steeled himself.

'*You* will need some kind of uniform and sword. Now, I have found a book with photographs. We must go over them together, you must decide. And then, you remember that Chinese tailor in Motomachi ...'

'I will not ...'

'But I am sorry, dear. I must insist. Everyone agreed, we *all* decided.'

'But I ...'

'It is for a good cause, remember that. It will be a big affair, a very big affair, for the club and for Kobe. The mayor and other Japanese dignitaries will attend. An invitation has even been sent to Prince Mikasa in Tokyo, and everything will go to charity. Now you cannot refuse. It is a small sacrifice to make, to help so many less lucky than us. Really Nate, you have no social conscience, and with all God has blessed you with too. You are becoming miserly in your old age.'

Peace. Please God. Peace. He thought of his wide, smooth office, the white space of it all, the comforting rattle of the typewriters. He thought of the new woman he had engaged for the shipping department, the sultry slant of her lips and eyes.

They both turned to the wall of Maud Bingham's room at the insolence of the crash. The splinter of china, the dead bounce of cutlery cut a passage through their words. Nate followed his wife to the door of his mother-in-law's room. 'You should have gone when she first called. How many times must I tell you? Now maybe she is dead.' But he did not wait to see.

From her bed Maud Bingham looked up at the sound of the opening door. It was Mama, she was sure, for when she blinked

Mama did not vanish in the annoying way Horace had the habit of doing. Mama walked on towards her, in the red velvet dress she had attended Prince Sadajiro Matsudaira's Musicale Tea Party in. The party was held on the fifteenth of each month at candlelight. The guests stayed drinking Japanese tea and *sake* and played on Chinese musical instruments until twelve at night. Maud had never been, but Mama had told her about it.

'Mama, did Prince Matsudaira play tonight on the *gekkin* or the *fue*?'

Mama was silent and closed the door firmly behind her.

'Mama, did you drink tea again in those beautiful cups, that had the distinction of never having been washed?'

But Mama was stern and angry. She picked her way carefully across the floor.

God give me patience, prayed Geraldine Cooper.

'Why did you not call me, Mother? Now there is egg yolk on the carpet, and a great deal more besides. Oh what a mess.'

'Call?' The face of her daughter, Geraldine, stared at her, very near. 'But I called and called. Yes, I am sure I called.' It seemed a long while ago, there was a curtain sometimes, like a mist, shutting off whole parts of her mind. Maybe it was yesterday she called, maybe she was mistaken. Everything evaded her since they came to this new house. And she could not understand, why was Geraldine in Mama's red dress? Or maybe it was really Mama.

'It is hers. It is Mama's dress.' She tried to sit up, for she saw now, it *was* Geraldine and she looked nothing as elegant as Mama had done. Geraldine appeared large and carnal; a carnivorous rose.

'You look like a harlot. Moreover, mutton dressed as lamb.'

For her head was throbbing suddenly with the injustice of it all, of the mists that cut her adrift, of the vanishing Horace, and Geraldine dressed in Mama's velvet dress. Such a horrid sight. And she remembered clearly now, she had called. She had. The egg yolk on the carpet was not her fault. So she spewed out the words again, the only defence.

'Mutton dressed as lamb, yes. Mama was tall and slim, very slim, and thirty-six when she wore that dress. Take it off. Take it off. I will not allow it.' Maud Bingham sat up, excited, and spat a lingering tea leaf into her hand.

Patience, God, please. Tears smarted in Geraldine Cooper's eyes. About her waist the whalebone pinched, and looking down precipitously she saw her belly, a red velvet shelf below her waist.

The clock on the wall showed nine. I have only an hour, thought Geraldine, to settle the old woman, to bath myself and change. For at ten she was due at Eva Kraig's, to present a donation to the orphanage from the Japan-British Society. And she had first to meet up with a reporter and photographer from the *Mainichi Daily News*.

The maid would clean the mess on the floor, but nothing would remove the stains on the carpet, or the words her mother just spoke. She turned towards the door. The world was a shabby, faithless thing, and much reduced about her. Offstage in her mind the committees flapped as rags in the wind, and sniggered at her back, like the old teeth in a glass by her mother's bed. She was sure of nothing but the lump in her throat.

8

Their cries were all around Eva now, like the cries of mice or birds. Little mice, she thought, little men, and ruffled the children's velvet heads. They dropped the heavy box of apples on the floor beside Eva, and looked up in pride and expectation.

The three-man-gang, she called them, Nabuo, Takeo and Jun, for they were always together, inseparable. Around them the other children waited, and behind them Sister Elaine and the helpers, Miss Kubo and Miss Mori. As expected Eva knelt and admired the rosy mound of apples in the box. The children had collected them the day before from the garden of old Mrs Okuno. Their small bodies pressed forward as Eva kneeled, fingers pointing and prodding individual fruits recognisable by a certain leaf, a maggot hole or woody stem. They recounted high-pitched stories of danger and success. She put her arms around them, and listened to their jumbled words. She wiped a running nose, replaced a sagging hairclip. The day before she had walked down the road to Mrs Okuno's, to see them there, in the old woman's orchard. The trees were heavy with fruit, and the children in their pale blue smocks swarmed beneath like bees. Eiko Kubo and Yoshiko Mori, amongst branches at the top of ladders, pulled at stubborn fruit. Below, Mrs Okuno, kimonoed and toothless, poked children and fruit alike with a stick.

There were only twenty-five children here, between the ages of five and twelve. They sent the more difficult ones to Eva from the Mission's new orphanage in Osaka. When it was built Eva stayed in the old house, caring for the children they left with her, commuting back and forth to the new Osaka home, to supervise medical arrangements there.

'Come now,' she said, standing up. 'You know what we have to do today.' She nodded to Eiko Kubo and Yoshiko Mori, to gather up the children. They were not much older than Akiko; like her they had grown up in the orphanage and stayed on. As children, they had clung together, and were no different now. Eva had a special affection for them. Red-cheeked Eiko Kubo was sturdy, with thick calves. Since childhood she had been the mouthpiece for tiny, alabaster Yoshiko Mori. Laughing, Eiko took hold of one of the boys.

'You're first, Nobuo.' The child pulled away with an angry shout and then grinned at her from the back of the queue, where he ran to the protection of Takeo and Jun.

'We will be first. We don't mind,' Yoshiko Mori said gently, holding the hand of eight-year-old Tami.

'I'm not afraid,' Tami announced to the boys. 'I shall be a doctor when I grow up. And I shall give you all injections. I won't let you run away.'

Eva turned into her surgery, where already the rows of needles and influenza vaccine were laid out neatly, and the children filed in behind her. Eva unscrewed the lid of a drum of toffee and a ripple of expectation passed down the line of children. She beckoned Tami to her.

The child walked boldly up. She was their motherly one, always rounding up younger children. She had been found three years before, abandoned in a subway. Her father was an alcoholic and her mother untraceable. Eva remembered the depressed state she had arrived in. It was these transformations that gave meaning to her life. She ruffled the child's thick hair.

'It doesn't hurt, Toshio, really.' Tami turned to the small skinny boy behind her who had drawn back in silent fear. His legs were still scarred by cigarette burns; he had been with them only six weeks. His mother had kept him locked in a shed and he had been found there by neighbours after she was placed in a mental asylum. His father quickly disappeared. Eva tried to reach him through the therapy of play and for some time now they had worked with the sand trays, and she watched him build within them his gaunt, horrific world. He looked at the needle and trembled. Yoshiko bent to soothe him.

Hurrying to his side Tami put a protective arm about him. 'I'll hold your hand. It won't hurt.' She pulled him forward.

'Let's give him his sweet first.' Eva unwrapped a toffee and popped it into his mouth, then took his small hand in hers. 'He's such a brave boy. Close your eyes and suck your sweet. There. It's over.'

'What a good boy.' Tami patted Toshio maternally and led the child away.

'Look.' Junko danced up. 'I'm a bumble bee.' She pirouetted on her toes. They called her '*Cho Cho*', butterfly, for she fluttered everywhere. She barely stood for the jab. Eva laughed and beckoned the next child.

Mostly they were docile, screwing up eyes and thrusting out arms, but little Kimiko cried in fear. Eva stopped and took the child on her lap. Her story was rather like Akiko's story. Her grandfather had been an American serviceman, whom her grandmother lived with for some years. Her mother, the product of that liaison, was a woman of the bars as her mother had been, and had no time for Kimiko. There were not many *konketsu* in the orphanage now, children of mixed blood. But in the beginning, they had been Eva's greatest concern, for after the war these children appeared with the American occupation, quick as a harvest of mushrooms. Such children were an unknown phenomenon in the closed and homogeneous history of Japan. Japanese society's response was luminous with one hard, bitter fact: they were unacceptable. Mostly these children, like Akiko, were adults now, lodged in menial niches on the periphery of society. But their marginalised plight had touched and concerned Eva, and involved her commitment when the war ended. She began to work with the mission amongst destitute women and their children, all victims of the American occupation. It had been a real problem at that time. She had adopted the child, Akiko, as a gesture of that concern. Akiko. Kyo. They pushed into her mind again. But she tried not to think.

Instead she looked at the faces before her now, eyes incised and black as mice, the small wet mouths. After all these years she had never grown accustomed to the callousness and sorrow that made each unwanted child; she tended to each as she had the first. They pushed forward the blind one now, Ruriko, blinded by syphilis before birth, and left in a hospital by a mother who discharged herself. Sometimes, when Eva thought of the children she visualised a dark river littered with battered bits of driftwood.

Ruriko lifted up her face and smiled with blank eyes. She pushed out an arm for the spirit swab, but her hand on Eva's knee clutched the white coat there. The child would leave them soon to go into a special home; she was six. She fingered the wax wrapping of the sweet in her hand as Yoshiko Mori led her away.

Nobuo, Takeo and Jun pushed before her, vying for who should be last. Eiko Kubo stepped forward to sort them out. Takeo had a mother in a mental home and an alcoholic father, Jun had been abandoned in a park, and Nobuo, the biggest one, had found his debt-ridden father hanging from a rafter, after his mother left home. Under Eiko's instruction they offered arms, took sweets and moved on. And soon it was finished, soon they were gone and the trail of feet and voices faded down the corridor. Usually at this time they would all be in school, but today was a holiday.

'Did the new child arrive?' Eva asked Sister Elaine, who waited behind in the surgery, after the children had gone. A boy of eleven, Kenichi, was to be added to the orphanage that morning.

'Yes, a little monster. They brought him all the way from Osaka in the orphanage bus, because no one would take him on the train. I hope we won't have trouble here.' Sister Elaine tightened her mouth.

'I expect we shall. We must prepare for it, and hope it won't last long.' Eva sorted through papers on her desk.

'He is not the kind of child I find easy to handle. And my concern is for his effect on the others.' Sister Elaine stood tall and thin, tight as a furled umbrella.

Eva looked up, her expression concerned. 'You seem very tired and anxious. I did ask you some time before if you felt well. Maybe a tonic is needed.' Eva had watched the woman in the six months she had been with the orphanage; the mission often sent one of their nuns to work at St. Christopher's. Immediately Eva had noticed the tension in Sister Elaine, like a spring that wound her taut.

'The Lord has been good enough to grant me fine health,' Sister Elaine said tightly. 'I am taking the older group of children for their apple picking. Am I to take that new child too?' she demanded.

'It would be an idea,' Eva said evenly. 'Be back by noon. Geraldine Cooper is coming to present a donation. She will want photographs with the children; she is bringing some newspaper people with her. The donation will buy us six new desks.' Eva smiled, but the woman stood waiting to go.

Eva watched her shut the door, and shook her head silently. She turned back to the paperwork on her desk, but found herself abstracted. And soon she saw them going out together, Akiko and Daniel, pushing open before them the high iron gate. For a moment Akiko's profile swung towards Eva, free of the dark fall of hair, then the gate shut upon them. From the distance that separates, even in love, Eva looked at the disappearing back of the child she called her own.

Her own. My own. Silently she had said the words to herself that first evening, looking at the child asleep in a box. An ugly stained cardboard box, with cheap red stencilled letters on its sides. No other child had come to her like that, on her doorstep, in a box. Outside the night had been closed and black, even though she had searched, calling to the dark. No voice answered, and the night had returned her to the child. And she saw that it was planned then. The box provided most things, two small jackets, a change of dress and underwear, some biscuit crumbs, a mouse made from a man's grey sock, already darned and worn before it was stuffed and embellished with button eyes. And Kyo's letter, crushed into a crumpled envelope that once held a gas bill, pinned to the child's dress.

Akiko, Autumn's child, an appropriate name, for her birthday was October, and the child was almost two. Eva had looked at the Japanese characters' meaning: Autumn and child. Crystal clear and bright, she had seen her fate etched there before her.

In the wide, round letters and misspelt English words of Kyo's letter there was no place for emotion. Kyo's stunted English spelt out only facts. From the bar where she worked near the military base she had struck up a relationship with an American serviceman. Akiko was his child, but the man left her before the child was born, returning without a word to the United States. One day he was there, the next he was gone, with neither warning nor contact address. At the base they would give her no information, and told her brusquely to get rid of the child, but it was too late. After Akiko's birth Kyo had tried to support the child, which had been hard. Now there was an opportunity for her, they wanted some Japanese girls in Bangkok, for a new cabaret opening there. Kyo was going. The child, Akiko, she would leave with Eva. She alone, Kyo knew, would care. She could do with the child what she wished, what she thought best. Put her up for adoption, Kyo said.

In the box the child had stirred, wedged uncomfortably against the sides. And Eva knew then, however hard she tried to find her, there would be no trace of the woman, Kyo. She had chosen to walk away. And there has been, of course, no contact until today.

9

Daniel focused his camera on the heavy roof behind the trees, and then followed Akiko. After a narrow approach, between scraggy pines and rickety houses they reached stone lions that guarded the shrine. The doors of a storehouse were open beyond. Pulled out from within was a festival float, like a ship in dry dock, surmounted by a huge drum. Two men in short *happi* coats, beat the vertical drum from either side, attacking rhythmically. Tendons stood out like oiled rope on their bare legs. Daniel took a photograph and allowed Akiko to lead him deeper into the crowd. Women and small children jostled about him, women with baskets of shopping and aprons still on. The drum pounded in his head.

'Each local shrine has its festivals,' Akiko said, the throb warming her face. Sun beat hard and flat on her hair, until it seemed fluid. He watched her denim skirt threading deeper into the crowd.

Sometimes now the sun went in and the shadows of clouds fell over the shrine. But the heat remained and the gnats droned on in a soft grey cloud beneath a pine. There was the close human smell of bodies, and the sudden odour of a woman's hair lacquer, or leeks in a basket of shopping. Japanese folk music blared from the mouth of a megaphone, attached to the branches of a tree. Strung above Daniel's head paper lanterns swung pink and white and red, their fragile globes crinkled like old women's faces. A child, its nose half buried in candy floss, bumped into his knees. He bent to steady the child, and the small boy's eyes met his own for a moment, widening in fear before he ran off. Daniel felt his own difference then, in the curious glances around him, although the mother of the child smiled a shy apology for the sticky stain upon his trousers.

They broke free of the crowd and came to an open area before a square makeshift dais at the centre of the courtyard with a canopy of red and white cloth. It resembled a gayly iced cake in the shrine yard. A group of matronly women danced upon it in a sedate ring, their hands moved smoothly, weaving patterns in the air. They wore identical *yukata* with a wave design at the sleeve and hem, red *obi* were folded on their backs.

'They're local women, come to dance today,' Akiko told him. Her eyes were thoughtful, her face a smooth pebble turned in upon itself. He saw isolation fitted her closely, like an armour, and wished he could find a way to her. She shaded her eyes against a blaze of sun released abruptly from a cloud. Her nails were small and perfect, on her neck was a soft brown mole.

'I haven't had candy floss since I was a child,' Daniel said seeing the stall after they left the dancing. She shook her head when he offered her some. He walked forward to where a crowd of children stood. A coarse-featured fellow in a grey peaked cap stooped before a tub, a circle of clear plastic was pegged in a curtain above the cauldron. Against its transparent sides Daniel watched stray strands of sugar harden and crack, in a delicate web. In the depths of the cauldron the man twirled a stick, collecting a soft cocoon. The children pushed their money forward and darted away.

Daniel stood, looking down into the whirling pot at the sugar, spinning and spinning its endless web. The gyration closed in on him, spiralling up. And he was back for a moment again within the cramped confines of his mind, so that he stared at the great muff of candy floss the man placed in his hand, wondering why he had bought it. He held it on his tongue and it melted gritty and sweet in his mouth.

'Have some,' he said, holding out the candy floss. 'There is so much. You bite from that side, I'll bite from this.'

At first she shook her head, but he insisted. She pushed her face forward reluctantly, reaching out with her mouth for the soft sugar. He watched it lie like gauze on her lip, until she licked it off.

'You've got some on your cheek, come here.' Carefully, he picked off the strand. She stood still, but lowered her eyes when he touched her. He could think of nothing to say.

'What's that?' He pointed to the water, to break the moment, too sudden to accept or understand. She looked up slowly then, and they turned towards the tank, hollowed out of one great stone. An ornate metal dragon curled sinuously upon one side, water flowed from its mouth into the tank. Long-handled bamboo drinking cups sat neatly, face down on the rim before it.

'It's water for purification. Here, dragons are harmless water spirits. Long ago they were often painted on ceilings as a protection against fire,' Akiko said beside him.

Sun struck the surface of the water; the tank brimmed and overflowed. Looking down he saw himself stare up out of the brown silk stone of the bottom. Beside him in the water the girl quivered and changed and found shape again, defying substance. Between them reflected the snowy mound of floss; behind, sun edged the rim of a cloud.

The pounding of the drum pulsed through Daniel's head. The shuffle of feet on the stage vibrated through the sound system beneath the beat of the drum, but the voices of the dancers were clear and high at the chant of the chorus. '*A yoi yoi yoi*', like the plaintive cry of a lonely bird. And for a moment there was Casey again, there was the river with its still, rich smell, closed and smooth, reflecting only the unperturbed sky, hiding in its belly Casey and the car. He shook himself free of the picture.

They found a seat against the pine and Akiko sat beside him. Beyond the jagged shapes of trees the sky was open and white and endless, the banks of cloud towering up like staircases. He wondered why he must feel so shut into the past, with his nightmares and his memories and wondered if it would ever end. He was conscious of the girl beside him.

'You must tell me about America. I know very little, but it was my father's country. I am always curious. All my life I have been trying to find him, in one abstract way or another. I should not, I know it is useless,' Akiko said. The words barely rose above her.

He saw then she hid a scar like him, one she could never forget. He saw she spoke with difficulty, as if each word shattered a secret life. Already he could tell she regretted having spoken, for her lips pressed hard upon each other. He knew how she felt, he wished he could tell her that he, like her, was separated for ever from other people, by something others could not grasp. But he could do no more than offer the candy floss.

'That accident. I killed two people, a man and a child.' It came out of him whole, like a stone. Casey's face came before him again, dripping still, a slimy weed entwined in his hair.

She shook her head, worried. 'No, it was an accident. Eva told me. An accident.'

But he did not want those feeble words again, divorcing him from himself, so that he existed free of his deed to other people.

'No. I killed them. I know it. I did.' He wanted to tell her, wanted her to know.

She did not speak then, beside him on the bench.

'You are the first person to whom I have said that.' For until now he had let them say all they wished.

Under the noise and the music there was a stillness now between them, a stillness he could almost touch. And he knew that in some soundless way the girl had entered and was there with him, in the stark, painful world of his thoughts.

10

'She has come. Mrs Cooper has come,' they informed Eva. She put down her pen on a list of accounts. The woman had come at the same time as the children, trooping back from the orchard. Eva walked resignedly to the visitor's parlour.

'Eva, my dear. Isn't this marvellous?' Geraldine Cooper engulfed Eva in an embrace.

'There will be more. Oh, much more. We have already started on the Christmas collection. I can safely say you may expect another donation in December.' For at intervals Geraldine Cooper rolled in upon the orphanage, a string of committees clattering in her wake.

'For what other reason are we here, if it is not to help those less fortunate than ourselves. I consider it my duty, the very least I can do. Now, I want that all down, I don't mind being candid.' Geraldine Cooper turned to a frail, young Japanese man with a notepad hovering behind. She sank into a cane armchair and accepted gratefully the glass of lemonade Yoshiko Mori offered on a lacquer tray. About her the basketwork creaked.

'I want the first photograph to be you and me, Eva. Don't you think so, my dear? In these two cane chairs, with the cheque nice and crisp between us, just here. And then some more with the children and Sister Elaine. Perhaps we can mention all that marvellous fruit they just picked, the dears.' Geraldine motioned Eva into the chair, and rummaged in her handbag for the cheque.

It was a large, soft-bellied bag with an opulent clasp, aptly reflective of Geraldine Cooper. She fished out scissors, a screwdriver, a compact and two postcards before retrieving the cheque. She waved it aloft, her plump face pink, like an ancient baby.

'From over there I think, from the left.' Geraldine waved the photographer into position with the red-talon of a fingernail. 'On my right of course I still have that nasty old scar where I fell against the roses around our front door.' In a mirror Geraldine snatched an anxious glance at her face, upon which time would soon wage its final assault. Then the flash bulb popped, and Eva blinked.

'It's all so kind, so kind,' she murmured, as the bulb flared again. Beside her Geraldine Cooper smiled fixedly through a stiff hedgerow of eyelashes, heavy with mascara.

'Nonsense my dear. My duty. And you know what a tender spot I have for you. An old softie, that's me.' Geraldine Cooper rapped Eva's knuckles playfully. 'Now off we go. A change of scene.' The chair creaked ominously as Geraldine rose, but she took little notice. She was used to such deferential murmurings, such justifications of her weight.

Why do I always allow this takeover, thought Eva. For a moment Geraldine appeared to resemble an inflated crepe paper rose or a broken shutter flapping in the wind. Eva sighed and smiled, resigned herself and followed. She could not dislike the woman, she was not given to that emotion, and Geraldine's kindness was always overwhelming. They reached the dining room door.

'Ah. The darlings. The dear ones. Here we are,' Geraldine threw open her arms, plunged into the room and moored herself amongst the apprehensive orphans, about to sit down to lunch.

She made first for the tables where the little ones sat. She condensed herself onto a small wooden chair, her hips overflowing its childish proportions. Reaching out she pulled the blind one, Ruriko, to her. Geraldine's flesh swelled and pressed about the child and Ruriko pulled back, her nose twitching as she breathed in the expensive scent of fern and musk. She put up a hand and touched a cheek. A soft touch within which Geraldine Cooper remembered and dissolved.

'The little blind one. Mariko. Of course.'

'Ruriko.' The child smiled.

'The darling. Of course.' Geraldine Cooper pulled the child onto her lap, pressing cheeks together, melting bones, gesturing to the other children. They held back, uncertain, until Sister Elaine gathered and grouped them about Geraldine. They blinked and one cried when the flash bulb popped. Undeterred, Geraldine Cooper unfolded herself from Ruriko's chair, and examined at the end of the tables the gleaming apples, washed and piled into blue plastic baskets. She turned one against the light in her hand, sniffing its fragrance. The camera flashed again.

Eva could see the pictures already, distorted and distant, awash in a sea of alien newsprint out of which only Geraldine Cooper's strength of will would survive. Still, she kept prominent the thought of the desks they would receive, as a result of Geraldine's cheque. She noticed the new child then, Kenichi, sullen before his food. He did not raise his eyes, he did not smile with the others, who were shyly attentive to Geraldine Cooper's small cries. He looked down at a dish of shredded radish and one sour pickled plum, shuttered within himself.

Such contempt was a challenge to Geraldine Cooper. She

made straight for the child, hovering above him like a strange plumed bird. She cooed and dipped and muzzled his crew cut head. The soft stubble of his hair parted beneath her chin. But stiff as a biscuit, he gazed at the buzzing of a grounded fly. He ignored Geraldine Cooper's administrations. The other children watched and waited, the moment stretched and snapped.

There was the quiver and fall of the chair, and the cry, wrenched from deep in the child and thrown up, all splinter and rag. Eva saw destitution then in his face, like an ugly bruise beneath the skin. He picked up the plate of radish pickle and sesame seeds, and threw it at Geraldine Cooper.

It splattered one ample breast and hung in limp yellow strands from the collar of her dress. The burnt black specks of sesame seeds were like ants upon her neck. Geraldine Cooper's face became that of an old and crushed pink doll. She trembled, she wobbled and sat down on a chair. Eiko Kubo sprang forward with a wet cloth and Yoshiko Mori rushed after the child. Eva herself picked the sesame seeds from Geraldine Cooper's neck, under her fingers the skin was soft as old kid gloves. The full crease of Geraldine's décolletage imprisoned a radish shred. It came away warm between Eva's fingers.

'It's our new one,' Eva apologised. 'He just arrived this morning. He is difficult, disturbed, they warned me about him. But I am so sorry for this.'

Geraldine Cooper gallantly reassembled herself, dabbing a handkerchief to her neck.

'Don't worry. I understand. It's all part of your wonderful work, my dear. I hold myself ready in life for most things, and the dress was due for the wash. Anyway, we were all finished, I think.' Geraldine nodded to the reporter and bit at a sesame seed on her lip. 'Fortunately, I like the taste of these things.' The seeds broke crisply between her teeth.

With appropriate noises and more fussings, Geraldine left the orphanage, waving a hand from her car. Sister Elaine looked meaningfully at Eva.

'I'll go,' Eva replied.

He had shut himself into a second floor storeroom. There were no locks on the door, and he had kicked Yoshiko Mori, who followed him into the room, tearing open the delicate skin of her shin. Even in the dark of the windowless space, his eyes were black as polished beans. In the bony sunken face Eva saw desperation, and knew he prayed as he picked his nose, crouching in the corner. Nothing would work but strategy, so she bustled in boldly and gave him a smile, and opened the cupboard above him wide.

'Clever boy. How did you know you were supposed to come here, that this was the first place I would bring you? For they didn't send much with you from Osaka, I expect they knew they were not your permanent home. You have had quite a number of homes, haven't you? But here it will be different. This is your real home, and we shall be your family. The first thing we give you are some nice new clothes.'

He crouched, terrified, and did not move. He was a big, strong boy and looked older than his age, standing taller than the other children.

'Now, this is one of the boys' store cupboards. This side are T-shirts and this side are shorts. Everyone chooses their own things, what they like best. You may have three of each for everyday, to begin with. There will be something smarter for when you go out.'

He threw her a derisive look, but his eyes ran over the folded garments.

'For your underwear and pyjamas there is not much choice. I'm sure you won't mind. It's all nice and new, but in another room. I'll get those while you choose from this cupboard.' Without a look she left him, switching on the light as she turned out of the room.

In the beginning, she remembered, it had taken so long with Akiko too. And there had been the same measured look in her eyes, the same terror jousting there. So that now such a look never roused Eva, but stilled her, and made her patience endless. Akiko too had run agitatedly backwards and forwards, her face smudged by fear and tears. But when she saw there was no escape, no hope, she became passive and would not eat. The third day it rained and rained, and in that deluge she had disappeared. Eva found her at last, sodden, awash with tears and rain, her voice worn thin by a darkness too dense to comprehend. Eva had carried her home, peeled off the wet clothes, wrapped the child in a blanket and sat her by an oil stove. The grey wet light of the room flickered and warmed and gave itself up to the glowing wick. And caught in that light the child's soft skin was the petal of a small pink bud. Her eyes gleamed; painful and resonant in the tracery of her tiny face.

Her own. The thought had filled Eva. Her own. She knew it then, and bent to kiss the child's hot skin. And at that moment in the firelight of the room it seemed they stared at each other out of a common emotion. But still it had taken much time before the child did not recoil, until there had been no more between them than a membrane of intuition. Her own.

Kenichi jumped at the sound of Eva's step. His arms flailed

above his head, trapped in the stubborn sleeves of a shirt, until Eva pulled it down. His hair was ruffled askew, then sprang again to its solid shape, like rice stubble after a harvest. He wrenched himself free, glowered and poked a finger up his nostril.

She had seen him first in the Osaka orphanage. 'He'll have to move on. It's your turn to try,' the Mother Superior regretfully stated. 'It's not often we fail, but we have so many here we simply haven't the time he needs. But I must warn you, he is such a strong child physically, he inflicts quite a punch in a fight, as we know to our detriment.'

He had sat at a low table, no other child near him. The rest were in easy groups, thumbing comics, crunching rice crackers, absorbed in a battered, flickering TV, all except Kenichi. His exclusion was clearly upon his own terms. Hunched above the table, he glued matchsticks doggedly into the lines of an obscure shape. All his will and need lay curved in the line of his backbone. Eva looked at the mute bodies of the other children and felt instinctively, in this one child, a strange and angular agony the others did not have. If only she could reach it. Remembering now, Eva observed him silently, as he faced her grimly from his corner.

'Is that the only T-shirt you want?' She looked at his ribs, now emblazoned with a racing car. They had told her about him. He had survived a family suicide, several years before. His father went bankrupt and to save his honour shuttered the house, and turned on the gas. They still happened often in Japan, this kind of suicide. At first they thought Kenichi too was dead, stretched out beside his brothers. Instead he survived, the only one; they left him with his memories. And they blazed before him now, turning his eyes to a mackerel gleam. Eva approached him.

'Shall we choose some others?' But he shrank back to a small tight ball in the corner, crouched into the seams of the room. She knelt before him.

'Or we can do it another time. We do not make you do anything here you do not want to.' She said it gently and saw he was nonplussed. But his stance was already set. He sprang up and, pushing past her, ran from the room. She heard his feet spill down the stairs. From the window of the corridor she saw him emerge into the playground below, and settle to a lonely exile.

11

Sister Elaine closed her copy of St Augustine's *City of God*, and replaced it on the shelf in her room, bare but for a bottle of cough mixture, The Gospels and her rosary. The night was black and silent, she could not sleep. From the open window came the sound of a cricket and the occasional frog. Across the road, from Eva Kraig's garden, drifted the scent of pink night flowers. The night, the sounds, the stillness of it all, formed a ring about her, waiting and watching, until she wanted to scream. She clenched her hands, pressing her lips together to control herself, her teeth cut into her flesh. She got up and stood by the window. Spindly iron railings gleamed in the porch light, the moon left a path across the bay, like the luminous trail of a snail. Her thoughts blurred and were tossed back upon her by the night. She feared she would not survive its judgment.

Turning from the window, she knelt beneath the crucifix on the wall above the bookshelf. But comfort did not come. God only stared at her, rigid and static, still. How long, she thought. Dear Lord, how long will you leave me like this, abandoned? Three years. Three years. How much longer can I go on?

She had been a school teacher in Ireland, not far from the town of Killarney in Kerry, where she had been born. It had not been until her late twenties that she thought of the religious life. 'I will go unto the altar of my God. Even unto the God of my joy and my youth.' For she was still young, still full and brimming, that first year as a postulant. The ugly clothes, the frugal life, the dishes of plain lentils and the jugs of cold water, these things she hardly noticed. The sun, from the stained glass windows of the chapel, falling mostly on aged sisters imprisoned in bathchairs, on the rheumatoid knots of praying hands, did not depress. She was young, she was full for sacrifice.

'But we shall have to see.' The Novice-Mistress had stared inscrutably into her face. Yet a year later she was clothed as a novice, and three years later took her vows.

'What do you desire?' the bishop asked her.

'Grace and mercy,' she replied.

She received the veil and the wedding ring and the thrice knotted girdle of poverty, chastity and obedience. And still the mysterious bliss followed her through the echoing cloisters to her barren, whitewashed room. Until one day she woke and found God observed her and turned His face away.

'The Dark Night of the Soul,' said the Reverend Mother in a pleasant professional tone. 'God does not hand Himself out like a free gift in a supermarket. I suggest a reading of St Anthony.'

St Anthony, St Basil, St Wilfred of Rheims, St James, and through the Liturgy of Hours, from Lauds until Compline. But each morning saw the same gritty wind cut about her on stone floors, a thin and shabby thing.

'Aridity,' the Reverend Mother conceded. 'A case of aridity. A common enough thing, though the symptoms are painful, and hard to bear. The blackness can be appalling, you may have to prepare for a very long time. Even I myself ... but well ... those who survive gain a purer faith. Later you may think yourself blessed.' Her voice was small and high, her face old and finely cracked, like ancient Chinese porcelain. She leaned forward kindly in her chair. From the window a cold winter light pushed between the soft pleats of her veil.

'More often than not there is a reason, my child. Can you find none in yourself? It would be best for you to tell me.' Pale eyes probed gently beneath wrinkled lids.

Sister Elaine hesitated. Outside, the world was bound by snow, the tall room was icy and echoing. She examined the whitewashed bricks of a wall and fought for a way to release it. For the memories moved in her raw and warm, but sealed tight still, imprisoned in her body.

They had let her go home when her sister Irene was killed, back to the farm in Kerry. They had brought her body back from Armagh, for that they knew would be her wish, to be buried in the green and peace of Kerry. In the old stone house the three coffins crowded the small front room, filling the air with the sharp scent of wood. The small boxes of the children lay either side of Irene, all killed in the senseless blast of an IRA terrorist bomb, on an innocent morning's shopping. Irene and the little one died outright, shredded and charred; six-year-old Tom lasted the night. They sealed the coffins immediately, for these were not bodies, simply remains.

Before the three coffins her mind had stopped. She stared

at the children's. Such little boxes, such little boxes. No other thought would come to her. And then and there the words of prayer had dried upon her lips. But the family expected the comfort of her vocation; she had offered them smooth easy phrases that helped not a single soul.

She was a twin sister, there had been that special affinity between them. Why was it not me, questioned Elaine, tossing each night in the small house they had both been born in. Sun set the gorse ablaze through the day and filled the thick green meadows. Why? Why did she take one path in life, why was I spared in another? We were born as one, we grew as one. The thoughts ran through her head, until her mind was full of holes. Part of her body seemed ripped away and sealed in the box with Irene.

'My child?' The old face of the Reverend Mother pulled her back to the present.

'My sister ... you know the way she died ... and the children ... so young and innocent ... for what purpose? I cannot accept it. And every day there are more ... it's senseless ... I ...' She stopped, her head thumping in sudden pain, words lost in a wave of bitter feeling.

'Ah.' The Reverend Mother sighed, and sat back sadly in her chair. But her words of comfort and wisdom passed flatly by Sister Elaine, unfolding no new dimension. The Reverend Mother watched her closely.

'It would be best I think to take the course of action, dramatic action and demanding work. You must go away from here. We must help the Lord to heal you.' She nodded under the cold light of the window.

And soon they had sent her here to Japan, and after six months in the Osaka mission, to Eva Kraig and St Christopher's in Kobe. She had felt the Reverend Mother's unseen sympathy, felt the support and taken new heart. And briefly there was an easing. Then the darkness once more engulfed her and lived with her day and night.

Now, in her small room in the orphanage, she dug the knuckles of her hands into her aching forehead. The seam of a floorboard pressed into her knee.

'Dear God. Dear God ...'

But only the black angry eyes of the new child, Kenichi, glittered in her mind. She saw Eva Kraig's smooth, fair-minded face taking its rational decisions, and the anger rose to her throat and struck like clappers in her mind. So that she trembled, her locked knuckles white with tension.

'Please God. Please God, not this ...'

12

Eva Kraig took down the pillow book of the courtesan Sei Shonagon, and read idly its quaint lists of tenth century charm.

'Unsuitable things: A woman with ugly hair wearing a robe of white damask. Ugly writing on red paper. Snow on the houses of common people. This is especially regrettable when the moonlight shines upon it.'

But the words only slipped before her and did not amuse. For her mind was still full of the morning's reflection, a blade of light that slit the darkness of the night. She could not sleep, but sat in the chair listlessly turning pages.

'Very dirty things: Slugs. The lacquer bowls in the Imperial Palace.'

She closed the book. Across the road in the orphanage the light in Sister Elaine's room still burned. But about Eva the sleeping house made no sound. In the black night sky of the window she saw only the sinuous expression that had been in Kyo's eyes. She put her head in her hands then, and thought of all the tomorrows.

It was no use, she could not sleep, she turned restlessly in bed. From far away the faint sound of the sea came to her, carried on the night. She got up and went downstairs. The house lay quiet about her. The moon sent long shadows off the trees across the deserted road outside and traced with grey light the graining of the corridor. The boards beneath her creaked. But the light was already on in the kitchen, filling the glass panes of the sliding door. Akiko sat at the table with a mug of hot milk and a biscuit.

'I couldn't sleep,' she said, but offered no reason.

'Neither can I.' Eva poured milk into a small pan, and when it had warmed sat down by Akiko. They did not speak, each involved with their thoughts; the woman, Kyo, lay heavy between them, unknown to each other.

Eva remembered then another night long before, when the old dog, Shiro, died. And the child would not sleep, but came down in the night, and Eva found her, distraught, beside the basket.

'He won't wake up. Is he dead? Is he dead?' Akiko had sobbed. Eva covered the basket with a cloth and took the child on her lap, searching for a way to make death acceptable. The sob and tremble of the child's body upset her deeply. She could not bear to see the hurt in Akiko's eyes, and more than the hurt, the loss. For it was in that state the child had come to her, it was the first expression Eva had seen on her face. She had wished to protect her from it always. Now she feared the blood mother Akiko would regain would bring only a greater loss. Eva had not the courage to ask about the letter. She held the warm milk on her tongue and did not look at Akiko.

How can I tell her, thought Akiko, for her mind and spirit were torn in two. Across the table Eva sipped from the mug of milk. Whatever her thoughts, they lay hidden behind the calm exterior of her grey eyes, the serenity of her expression was rarely disturbed except by the warmth of her smile. But her eyes could read a silence, though her mind resisted as always quick judgments, assessing things clearly. Few people did not respond to her with liking or respect. Released from the severity of its daytime coil, her hair was gathered softly at her neck. Akiko watched and paused in the constriction of her own narrow thoughts, feeling a sudden rush of warmth. Without Eva, she knew, her life would have been a very different affair. The continuity, security and love Eva had always offered, would not have been found with the woman who now claimed to be her mother. She knew it instinctively. It was the touch of Eva's love that had shaped her life so surely. She knew it and was grateful. And yet, the need to know more about her blood mother consumed her.

Twice, when she was a child, Eva had gone to America, and Akiko stayed in the orphanage. But each day she crept back to the house and stared through a window at the silent room inside, thick with an unfamiliar stillness. It was filled with Eva's absence. She had never forgotten that dead look of the house without Eva. It had terrified her.

And again, the day after her tenth birthday, they had walked along the narrow beach, searching for sculptured driftwood and shells. They had gone a long way before climbing up to the road, and Eva had tripped there, falling back, hitting her head on some rocks. She lay unconscious, and terror filled Akiko. She is dead, she thought, and the world had stopped about her. Running to the nearest house, she brought them back to Eva. But she had known in that moment the depth of her love for Eva; no one could take her place. And yet now, the need to know her true origins devoured her, whatever it might bring.

'Come, we had better go up,' Eva said, standing. But at the door Akiko turned suddenly to hug her, feeling the comfort of Eva's body, as she had when a child. Words of affection and gratitude came to her, but she could not form them. 'Thank you for everything, always.' It was all she could say.

'Akiko.'

In the dark kitchen they stood still and close, unable to put into words the love that enveloped them both.

13. Friday

Arthur turned up the music. I shall not be defeatist, he thought. I shall not give in to negative thoughts.

'One two. One two. A little more stretch, Mrs Greenly. Swing to the left, Mrs Dent. Lower, Mrs Tanaka.' He roared to the Friday morning keep fit class he organised for the club. For immediately after they retired him at Murdoch and Hack, he sought to expand his numerous interests to pack the empty day.

'Up down. Right left.' He swung his arms about, feeling the flex of his own pliant muscles. The thin hard drop of piano notes filled the ballroom of the club and sweat trickled comfortingly down Arthur's back. He always welcomed the issue of sweat, like a physical manna given up by his body in thanks for the care he relentlessly gave it. The more he sweated the more satisfied he felt, the more right seemed the day with himself, especially now in retirement. The daily servicing of his body had become the obsession of these six months. A day of missed exercise and depression descended.

He had come early that morning to the club, and in spite of the sudden change in weather, enjoyed his swim in a deserted pool and the spotting of rain on his already wet flesh. He swam sixteen lengths, then strode in for the class, light and fresh in T-shirt and shorts. He was proud of a physique younger men would envy. During warming-up exercise he surveyed the young women, over-fleshed and flabby muscled, and felt suitably superior. But he enjoyed the class.

Swinging his arms to the chandelier on the ceiling, he thought of the changes he had seen in the club. Before the war it had been inconceivable to think of women here, bouncing about energetically; it had been a men's club. Even his own scanty attire would not have been tolerated, for ties and coats had been de rigueur. Only, he remembered, during the great flood, when the club was under water, had word been quietly passed that shorts were permitted during the emergency. But hats were still essential and they kept their sun helmets on. Topees were the mark of the old-timer, setting wearers apart from new arrivals.

On the committee of the club, Arthur organised the sports facilities. Now, in retirement, he gave himself to it wholeheartedly. Recently he had tried to resurrect The Ancient

Order of Mountain Goats, a select but obsolete fraternity of walkers in the first quarter of the century, who had roamed the Kobe hills. New goats nowadays were not easily enticed. The Harriers, which Arthur also supported, with their energetic paper chase, bawdy songs and beer, clearly held the upper hand. The club's Ancient Order of Mountain Goats was sadly no more than two stoic Lieutenant Goats, and a third commanding member, The Bell Goat, Arthur.

'Up, Mrs Williams. Up, Mrs Brown.' The honky-tonk music of the tape recorder struck faster in the ballroom. In black leotards the two rows of women kicked out their legs like a straggling loose-thighed chorus line. Arthur shot out orders and the women jumped to obey, panting and shiny with sweat. Before them Arthur turned the exercise into graceful fluid movements, and afterwards the women crowded round him, laughing and envying. He enjoyed their feminine attention and his Friday morning was pleasantly passed.

But the afternoon stared at him the moment he entered his home. He passed his old sun helmet, hanging in memory of former times, from the antler of a deer head in the hall. Because of the rain and a virulent virus that had claimed most of his troop, the weekend Boy Scout camp on the slopes of Mount Maya had been abandoned unexpectedly. He had planned it to fill the days looming ahead. He was secretly terrified of smaller children, but older boys he enjoyed. He had looked forward to the camp, to the smell of earth when he woke in a tent, to tin mugs of burnt cocoa and charred potatoes baked in the embers of a fire. And the boys with their uniforms and quick hands and minds, returned him to his own scouting days. Only the size of his uniform differed in the troop.

He made a cup of coffee and sat down at his desk, and turned his mind back to the history of the club. He wrote a heading for the first chapter.

'Growth of the Foreign Settlement: By evening of that first day in Kobe Port, rows of canvas shanties had been erected on the Concession ground, while a few Japanese houses had been taken over and were already in full swing as grog shops. So that, long before dark, this peaceful Japanese town was converted into a place where hell seemed to be let loose, with Japanese and Europeans rolling about drunk, fighting, bawling and chasing women ...' Arthur copied carefully from a book entitled, *Links in My Life on Land and Sea,* written by an early English traveller.

Rain spat lightly on the window. In the garden the topiary bushes of holly and privet gleamed wetly, like large one-legged metal birds. He saw the belt of rain coming towards him off the bay, it veiled the town, then quickly the hill. He watched it touch the garden, thrusting noisily between branches and leaves. A damp praying mantis climbed the window through crystals of rain. He observed its fleshy underside, like a fat green pod of peas.

On the corner of his desk the fragments of vase, broken yesterday, made a neat stony pile. He had not thrown them away. Looking at them he remembered and it seemed even now his bones would melt again. I shall die, he had said. I shall die. He remembered his words so long ago, for his mind had burst with light. But she had only laughed and bent to touch his body. Kyo.

About him the house dripped morosely, filled with stagnant smells of drains and mould and rotted wood, the solitary remnants of bachelorhood. I should have married, he thought,

I should have had children. For what is there left and who will
care? It will be like Spencer. He shook himself at once. For these
were the thoughts that buried Spencer, these were the shoes
without laces, the mangy dog, the braces buttoned with safety
pins. He, Arthur, was not a man to give in so quickly. And
besides, he had History and Spencer had not. He picked up his
pen and began to write, and the woman, Kyo, was there in his
mind again. He sighed and sipped his coffee, for what good did
it do to remember, and determinedly bent his head to his work
again. Outside, the rain dripped on.

14

Akiko turned her face up to the light rain and ran ahead of Daniel
on the beach. The wind followed, rushing down stone passages
between concrete ballasts, heaped up as a breakwater against the
sea wall. Something new in her ebbed and flowed; she was one
with the sky and the sea and the rain. The wind took hold of her
hair, slapping it about her eyes. She had woken that morning and
seen the swollen rain-filled sky, and the pale undersides of leaves
stirring restlessly in the trees. Overnight the season had changed.
Later they had come down together to the beach.

'It's so ugly,' Akiko told him. 'There used to be sand before
they put all that concrete down. There is only somewhere to
walk because the tide is out. Once it was nice. Eva and I used
to walk here often.'

He nodded, agreeing, seeing the ugly dredging works, the
modern fishing pier and the monstrous triangular concrete
ballasts piled up in a wall behind him.

'Those are oyster beds,' Akiko pointed. 'It used to be nice: the sea, the sand and the oyster beds. And that's the Coopers' house. They're important people here, amongst the foreign community.' Akiko pointed to a house some way down the beach, set back across the road on its own. A high stone wall and the dull gleam from its copper roof was all that could be seen.

Akiko turned and began to run. The gritty shingle pressed between her toes, the crash of the waves rushed in her ears. The salty spray stung her face and left the taste of brine on her lips. The dark shapes of ships dotted the sea, the sky was like slate, with clouds moving quickly across it. She shouted behind her to Daniel. Wind ripped the voice off her lips and flung it aside. She clutched an umbrella, holding it high above her head against the drizzle. There was something special within her since yesterday, since he had told her those secret things, thrust up from the darkness of his mind. Things he had told nobody else.

Turning, she saw him coming towards her, bent and battling against the wind, his jeans rolled up his legs, bare feet wet and gleaming. He carried his shoes in his hand, socks stuffed into them. The black umbrella was lopsided and flopping upon its broken rib. Soon he was there beside her, and she smelled the damp of his shirt and felt the warmth of his breath on her face.

'There are still a few old rocks left, that I always used to climb over.' She led the way to the smooth flat slabs of stone and sat down. In her mouth was the taste of salt; the wind whistled in her ears. He stood above her, silently looking down. The wind came at them fiercely in a sudden flurry, and his umbrella blew inside out and flapped like an old black crow. He stood helplessly beneath it, his hair moving wildly about his face. She laughed and together they pulled the old umbrella back upon itself. At their feet an empty sardine tin and the remnants of a towel waited for the tide.

'There'll be no more summer after this,' she said, looking at the wide sweep of it all. A wave gathered seething along its crest, and crashed upon the shingle. A small boat lifted and rocked, tethered to a stump of wood. And she thought already, what shall I do when he is gone? For it was, even then, unthinkable. Something unravelled within her, something immeasurable and slow, like a great spreading shadow that grew and grew. So that she closed her eyes and dared to say it, because there was nothing to lose, nothing before her, and behind only unbending shapes of her own life.

'It will be strange when you are gone.' In the words she saw her own reflection, dark and obscure, like a shape in old glass.

'I'll be here for a while. I shan't go away so soon.'

'I ... I just mean, it will be lonely. I don't often have someone to talk to, like this.'

'You must have friends?' he said.

'Not really. There is Eva, of course. And the orphanage, the work, we're so busy always. There never seems time for much else. The foreigners, they come and go here. Nobody stays long enough for a friend. And the Japanese, well ...' In her mind was the crumble of something decayed and old. How could she explain, the hot skewered rice cakes, the empty desk, the child with flaxen braids? It was nothing he would understand. The forms in her life were stiff and still, and yet she wished to tell him, those things she had not spoken of. She wished to give as he had given, the dark contraction of her spirit.

'It is difficult here, as it is nowhere else, for somebody like me ... being half American, half Japanese.'

'There are plenty of people like you in the world. Why should it raise difficulties, emotional divisions maybe, but otherwise you're lucky. You sit on the fence, you belong to both sides.' He looked at her gently.

But she ached in the silence between the things she wished to unfold. 'In Japan it is different. You are here just a few days, what could you know? How can I explain?' She turned to him earnestly, her face thin in the gritty, windy morning. 'The Japanese feel themselves a race apart. This you must understand. I love Japan. I was born here of a Japanese mother. I have grown up here. And in spite of Eva I feel Japanese. The mirror tells me so each morning. I see my eyes, I see the shapes that make myself. I want to be Japanese. But I am not and never can be, because there is no place for me here. In the eyes of the Japanese I am an unthinkable adulteration; I do not belong to them. They have told me so in many ways, again and again.' She turned from him and looked at the phosphorous sea, her face still.

'And I understand their point of view. It is not discrimination, as any Westerner would immediately say. It is simply a fact of Japanese life. The foreigner is always the foreigner, the Japanese is always a Japanese. And knowing that it is unthinkable they should accept me, I am not bitter. I cannot say this is right and this is wrong. There is simply the Japanese way of thought and other ways of thought. But it makes me sad, for I feel very much alone. If it was not for Eva I don't know what would have become of me. I am one of the lucky ones. After the war there were many like me, but we have grown up. In some unhappy way this country has absorbed us. Most of the children I grew up with in the orphanage were of mixed blood but, in spite of education, they have been able to get no more than menial work. Eva tried hard for them all, but even to get them those jobs was an achievement. Some went for adoption to the States, and they are happy there, I know. One or two studied very well, but even with qualifications they are rejected here. Now there is a crop of children from international marriages. The Japanese study and travel abroad these days, which was not allowed before. So there are marriages, and children again. They are not orphans, and their social standing is much better than mine, they don't face the same kind of rejection. And yet it is there still. They are regarded as interesting curiosities, mostly they go to international schools, and take their non-Japanese side and are absorbed abroad again.'

'But Japan is very much part of today's world. It must adapt, change?' he asked. But she shook her head.

'The whole history of Japan is a history of isolation. They were never invaded until the last war. The very structure of society here is a protection against change. Everything may seem modern and westernised, but it's superficial. Socially, things have not changed as much.' She was empty now she had told him. She did not often speak at such length or with such emotion.

'You should come to America, you would be accepted for yourself there. Eva should have brought you long ago,' Daniel told her.

'In all the years she has only been once or twice herself, as you know. She is too absorbed here, nothing else matters to her. She brought back a photo of you once, she has it on her dressing table. I used to look at it when I was young, and dream all kinds of dreams, about my father, about America.'

'But you should come.'

'I'm not adventurous, in spite of all my dreams. America to me is an unknown place. What would I do there? It frightens me.'

'Oh no,' he said, but her face was serious and moved him.

'Sometimes I think what if anything ever happened to Eva, what would I do here then? Would I even want to stay? I dare not tell Eva but, as much as I love her and the children and enjoy the work, I am not filled with the same dedication Eva is. I grew up in the orphanage, it is all I have known. Yet sometimes it all comes down on top of me. I don't feel I can stay there the rest of my life. But I should be ashamed to tell Eva of the things I dream of: music, laughter, just movement and ... life. All the things Eva has no time for. Sometimes on the television there are pictures of people, singing and dancing. I wish I could go out and join them. They are people like me, my age. But even if I could I wouldn't know how. It is like an affliction in me.' She looked down at her hands.

'What of your mother? Do you know anything about her?' he asked gently.

She was silent, staring at her hands, yet he saw the flicker in her face, like a ripple in clear water. She shook her head.

In spite of herself Akiko felt the nearness of Daniel then, like a sharp, sweet ache in her bones. He placed a hand on her shoulder, turning her gently around. Before him her face did not move. For a moment the beating wings of a bird overhead parted the wind and rain. He bent to kiss her then.

15

They walked back in silence. There was both nothing and too much to speak of. Coming towards them down the hill people bent against the weather; in deep gutters each side of the road was the noisy swill of rainwater. They pushed their open umbrellas before them up the hill. Daniel stopped beside her then and took her arm, and together they walked on.

She remembered the letter again, and shut her eyes, gripping Daniel's arm tightly. On her lids was the comfort of the rain, beside her he was warm and sure. He bent towards her, sensing she was bothered by something. His hair was damp on his forehead, damp and flat and very near her own, one brow arched with beads of rain. He pressed her arm in silent question, and barely caught her voice above the swirl of wind.

'She said, "Sometimes I like to hope you think of me".'

'Who said that?' he asked.

'My mother.' She released it in a breath and knew at last she had shared that iridescent fragment of a word. 'I had a letter from her. Soon I shall tell you about it. But not now.'

Daniel placed an arm about her shoulders and they walked on, silent, their umbrellas locking sometimes before them against the rain.

Through the day the wet fell on leaves and stones, until they were polished and smooth. The wind continued restlessly, tossing about like an irritable sleeper. In the orphanage the electric light shone above the younger children, back from nursery school, as they folded origami paper cranes. Akiko slid her nail along the creases of magenta paper, opening wings, moulding a beak, directing short, clammy fingers on which glue curled in a grimy skin, daubed with coloured inks.

Against the dark sky the windows of the orphanage were sodden. Outside, the spiked fingers of a palm swayed and dipped. At three-thirty Akiko handed over to Eiko Kubo and went to Eva's office. They were waiting for her there with mugs of tea and thick slices of raisin cake. Sister Elaine stood by Eva, who was seated at her desk.

'I am afraid I cannot agree,' Sister Elaine said, as Akiko entered the room. 'I know how you feel, I share your hope and constant optimism. But this is quite monstrous. We cannot allow it. First Mrs Cooper and now *this*.'

Eva was silent. She pursed her lips and did not reply. Sister Elaine continued. 'That Kenichi ...' Sister Elaine crossed herself quickly. 'I feel it my duty to say, I think that child is a dangerous element in our orphanage.'

'What did he do?' Akiko asked, sitting down beside Daniel, who addressed a letter on his knees.

'Do? He had a fight with Nobuo. He pushed him downstairs, I saw it. Nobuo was concussed. I have just returned from the hospital with him. Yesterday he bit me, look,' Sister Elaine thrust out her wrist on which lay a small bud of broken skin. Her cheeks were pink and behind her, rain drummed on the windows.

'He's like a bit of taut string. The others were teasing him, I believe,' Eva said quietly. She looked at Sister Elaine in a worried way. 'We must give him more time. Most of the children here come from very disturbed circumstances, as you know. We must show patience, we must win their trust. Unfortunately, there is always the risk, in a house full of children, of an accident such as today's.'

'Well, I am afraid I can do nothing more with him. He has locked himself into the lavatory, and will not come out. He has been there three hours, since the time of Nobuo's fall,' Sister Elaine replied stiffly.

'I'll go after my tea. Don't worry, Sister Elaine.' Eva watched the woman nod curtly and leave.

'Perhaps I shouldn't have taken him, perhaps she is right. But somehow I felt ...' Eva trailed off uncommunicatively. There was something the matter with Sister Elaine. Eva saw it there in her voice and eyes, something compressed and deep. She looked at the square of dark window, reflecting bars of light and their faces. Beside her the telephone rang. She heard the voice, but there was nothing she could do. 'Akiko.'

The wire stretched short and tight between them, Akiko pulled her chair forward to reach it. But she knew even before she heard the voice, before the words uncoiled, one by one in her head, for she had been waiting. She knew that now.

'You will find the address easily. Between the Shinseiki Cabaret and the Ikuta Shrine. I would not ask you ... but I am ill ... Akiko ...'

'Yes,' she said. 'Yes.' It was all she could say. No other word would come. She knew they watched her as she replaced the telephone. She said nothing and their silence grew furred about her, demanding. In her mind the world was splintering, she did not want the darkness of their apprehension. She stood up and her body trembled, her voice shook. She pushed her chair back. 'I'm going out. I have to go out.'

Eva spoke first. 'Was it her, Akiko? Was it Kyo? Your mother?' For the first time the name lay open between them.

But still Akiko could not tell them. She nodded and did not

look into Eva's face. She turned towards the door.

'You cannot go now, Akiko. Not in this weather, Akiko ... they say a typhoon is coming ...' Eva half started from her chair.

'I'm going, I said. I'm going.'

Eva could find no words. She sat down in the chair again. Akiko's eyes were slim like her mother's, determined.

'It's not far, I'll be back soon. There is no need to worry,' Akiko said more kindly, filled suddenly with power. She turned again to the door.

'I'll come with you.' Daniel stood up decisively.

'No.' She flared, striking out with the word, their fears suddenly like nets about her. She wanted to be on her own, to touch the untouchable without witness. It was hers. Hers. No one must take it from her, no one must touch it. She had waited all her life.

'Nevertheless, I'll come. I'll wait around while you meet your mother. I'll not bother you.' He took a step forward. Eva looked at him gratefully. Akiko pursed her lips and turned quickly from the door.

Eva stared at the back of the girl. Suddenly in the shape of her calf, in the curve of her cheek, Eva saw Kyo and closed her eyes, and forced down the fear that was like a malaise. She sat for some moments in the silent room after Akiko and Daniel had gone. Then forced herself to walk to the door, and the problem of Kenichi in the lavatory.

The rain had stopped. There was no sun, just a strange dense light in the cooled, stirred air; the wind had dropped. In the sudden lull a moth fluttered low over a wet patch of grass. The playground of the orphanage was strewn with a wet mush of leaves. Akiko shut the gate behind her, not caring if

Daniel came or not. But soon she heard it swing again, and his footsteps follow on the road, hurrying to catch up. Taking no notice she made her way quickly down the hill. Over the bay the light was a bar above the horizon; within it a dark bank of cloud dissolving again to mist, sweeping towards the town. Studded with ships the bay was now grey as stone, whipped white with small waves, as if it had turned to quartz. A wind began low in the trees again.

She hurried on beneath the umbrella, listening to the soughing of the pines, looking up at their sombre patterns scratched upon the cloud-filled sky. Nothing could alter the knowledge that weaved its way towards her now. Nothing could alter the change it would bring about in her. So she paused and, still silent, allowed Daniel to walk beside her.

16

Drinking his tea, Arthur Wilcox took up the book of haiku and read:

A warbler
In a grove of bamboo shoots
Growing old, sings.

Hurriedly he shut the book. Then paced the floor, undecided. Outside the rain had briefly stopped, but a low wind continued, breathing restlessly, stirring foliage. The bay was marble veined with the spume of waves, spotted with ships, the clouds were gunmetal grey. The thought of the long evening, wet and lonely, seemed unbearable. He decided to go to the library at the club, to look for material for the centenary book. He would poke around upon a ladder, among the upper shelves. Who knew what he might find.

17

The sky was dark as iron, rain emptied down and the wind came in flurries, beating the wet about them. She walked close to Daniel. Rain drummed the bowl of the umbrella, dripped in streams from its ribs, and was blown again upon them. She tightened on the comfort of Daniel's arm. There were few people on the streets.

The road began at the lower gate of the Ikuta Shrine. On one side was a huge red lacquered *torii* arch, wet like patent leather now, and on the other was the dome of the Shinseiki cabaret and Turkish bath. From there, the narrow road turned upwards. There were some eating places, coffee shops and small boutiques, but mostly bars. Above them the street lights were warming up and mixed with the neon lighted names of dubious bars. They reflected like wounds; crimson, orange and purple in the sleek, sodden surface of the road. A slippery dusk was descending, and already the bars began to stir, a light behind a curtain, a fluorescent sign bursting into life above a door. Beyond their silent exteriors Akiko sensed another world. She swallowed hard and walked on, determined.

A blade of light slit the shutter of the window. Club Starlight and Bar was looped in silver above the dead black door. A blue plastic garbage bin and two empty beer crates huddled beneath the window, the large condenser of an air conditioner stood beside the door. The place was no more than ten feet wide.

'I will wait for you there, in that doorway,' Daniel said.

She nodded, unable to speak. The wind blew hard against her face, cold and wet with rain. She stepped forward and the door opened easily.

Two men and a woman sat before a bar counter, their expressions colourless as glass as they turned to stare at Akiko. A singer with an upswept hairdo filled the screen of a television, hooked high above the bar. Her voice warbled out, filling the room. The lighting was the low red glow of tulle shaded lamps on a passage of red wall. The door shut behind her and the walls seemed to close in about her. Akiko smelled her own clean smell of rain, like something indigestible in this low-lighted crimson belly. The raincoat dripped wetly on her ankles. The two men and a woman continued to stare at her. The men were rough types from the underworld. They wore the gangland uniform of garish clothes and permed or close-cropped hair. One wore a stomach binder beneath a thin shirt. The other slurped whisky loudly over ice, the amputated finger of gang allegiance hooked about his glass. They sprawled on plush red chairs rubbed thin about the seams. The woman leaned on the bar, in a slit-sided dress of peacock satin, her mouth a violet welt in her face, her body arched at the counter like a hard green reed. Akiko looked at her, wondering, not wishing to believe. The air was thick with the smell of whisky and drains.

A bartender emerged from a door behind the counter.

'What do you want?' A black bow tie moved with his Adam's apple.

She pushed herself to speak then, looking at the woman. But it was not her.

'Kyo?' she said. 'Upstairs.' And thrust out with her chin in the direction of some stairs. She moved away to a juke box, a coin dropped loudly in the slot.

It was a dream, and her body was scarcely flesh. She took a step forward to the narrow stairwell in the wall.

'Wait,' the woman at the juke box called, her eyebrows thin as razor wounds. She disappeared upstairs, her high heels echoing back to them. From the juke box came the sudden lash of music. The men stirred and exchanged incoherent remarks, laughing lewdly, watching Akiko. One held up a glass.

'A drink? Come here.'

Her stomach grew tight and she fixed her gaze on the television, and its jerking obsessive flow of images. The men continued to call her. On the television a commercial ended, the weather news flickered before her. The men's voices sounded in her ears, coaxing and salacious. The television droned on.

'Powerful Typhoon 21 cut across Kyushu early today killing seventeen persons and leaving scars from ferocious wind and torrential rain in its wake, disrupting land, sea and air transportation over the Kyushu area. The typhoon, packing winds of 50 metres per second, is gaining speed and has changed course in a north-easterly direction. The typhoon is expected to hit Osaka at nine o'clock this evening if it maintains its present speed of 90 kilometres an hour. Evacuation procedures have already started in the Tenoji area of Osaka where the eye of the typhoon is expected to ...'

'Pour her a drink on me.' The words were thrown from one end of the room to the other. The bartender smiled with one side of his mouth. Under his hand she watched the glass turn solid amber, and looked quickly up at the screen again.

'... all flights cancelled, railway services suspended. All residents in the Kansai area are warned to return home. We will continue to ...'

The woman clattered down the stairs again.

'Go up,' she said. 'Left at the top.'

The stairs were steep and awkward, the smell of drains rose up coarse and rich as she began to climb, and her heart beat fast behind her ribs. The door to the room was open, and already she wanted to retreat. Instead, she pushed herself to step forward and enter the room, and gaze down at the woman sitting on the bed.

They looked at each other silently. And within Akiko, every thought dissolved to shapelessness.

'So,' said Kyo, very slowly. 'Akiko.'

There were no words, just a numbness in her mind. Already she wished to see no more. From the body of this woman she had been made. From the body of this woman she had been born. The ugliness closed in upon her.

'Sit down.' Kyo made room on the side of the bed. A thin sheet was pulled loosely across her hips, and her shoulders were bare above a beige satin slip. She was colourless, the tone of yellow marble. Only her hair, coarse and dishevelled, was a bright copper red that darkened at the roots.

'I am ill, as I told you. I would not have called you otherwise. Or maybe I would have. To see how you turned out.' Kyo scrutinised Akiko.

A large mirror ringed by raw light bulbs, multiplied the room and Kyo on the bed. Before it a table was littered with cosmetics, and a chair was heaped with clothes. Pushed against a wall was a low metal-legged table and some cushions. Bottles and empty glasses were strewn about the floor, as if there had been a party and nobody had cleared away.

'There is some whisky in the bottle there.' Kyo had followed her eyes. 'Give me a drink. I need it. Seeing you. There, take this glass.' Her voice had a rough, cracked edge. She sat up in bed, her chest flat and bony beneath the satin bodice.

'I didn't do too badly. You're a pretty girl. Could be even prettier, if you used more cosmetics.' She tilted her head to one side, looking at Akiko. 'A darker lipstick, some eye shadow. And you don't pluck your eyebrows right. But we've plenty of time for that.' She took a gulp from the glass Akiko gave her.

'That's better. Good as a man inside you.' She closed her eyes and leaned back upon the pillow, then flicked them open again.

'You're shocked, of course. By me, by all this. I can see it on your face. What did you expect? Can't you speak? Don't you have a tongue?' She sat forward and peered closely into Akiko's face. 'Joe, his name was Joe. Bastard. You've got his nose. Left me when I was seven months gone. Foreign bastard. They murder you laughing, men.' She held the tumbler of whisky to the light bulb hanging from the ceiling. It glittered, bronze. 'I shouldn't down this stuff like I do. They told me at the hospital. But what other way is there? Tell me. It's my best friend. Doesn't do to see things too clearly. Doesn't do to think about things. Yes, you can look. You can look. But that's life. Life.' She shrugged and turned down the corners of her mouth.

'But let's get back to you. I am ill. You can see I'm ill. And I am your mother. You know it now. Maybe I should have come back to you before, I thought about it often. But what good would it do, I always said. I did well, leaving you with that Englishwoman. She looked after you, didn't she? I can see it.

She's a good woman. I knew she would look after you. But it's not too late. I have come back to live here in Japan. We'll make a home together now. And you'll help me, won't you? You'll look after me? For I am ill. I don't know when I shall be able to work again. But I have a plan. Chieko, that's her downstairs, she's a friend, she's given me this room here, I can stay for a while, but not forever, of course. Chieko's all right, and she's made money, enough to buy herself this bar. But we're not all so lucky. Look at me.

'Listen, someone has to help me. And I am your mother, nothing can change that. No adoption, nothing. You were born from my flesh and blood. I am your mother. And you're a pretty girl. I knew you would be. We'll live together, as I said. And I already spoke to Chieko. She'll find you a job, you can earn a lot with a face like yours. Much more than you'll ever get at that orphanage. I know where the money is. And I can teach you things. I know all kinds of people, I ... Akiko ... Akiko ...'

She stumbled over the debris on the floor. A bottle tipped and stale beer the colour of urine spilt over her foot and streamed foaming at the edges onto the tatami matting. The narrow walls of the stairwell guided her down.

'Akiko.'

The stale red cave received her again, and she ran towards the door.

'Akiko.'

An arm came down before her face, barring her way to the door.

'Your drink,' he said. 'You haven't had your drink. You're a pretty girl. We must get to know each other.' The man grinned, his face near her own, his breath corroded by liquor. Through the thin muslin of his shirt she could see the hair of his armpits, and she felt his hand on the back of her neck. He brought the glass near her, pressing it to her lips. The liquid was sharp and quick on her tongue and stung her in the throat. She began to cough. The man laughed, his hand moved to her shoulder and held her so she could not move, his body pressed against her.

'Leave her. Leave her alone.' Kyo pushed the man away, angry. And stood clenched and ready, naked beneath the satin slip.

'Kyo.' The man laughed coarsely, and moved towards the woman.

'Don't be jealous, Kyo.' He pulled her by the low neck of her slip towards him. Kyo laughed suddenly, half turned and thrust Akiko towards the door.

She looked back as the door swung shut behind her. But through the closing slit there was only the glimpse of Kyo's naked leg against the trouser of the man.

The horror surged up in Akiko then, tears pricked her eyes. Already her flesh was something dirty and diseased.

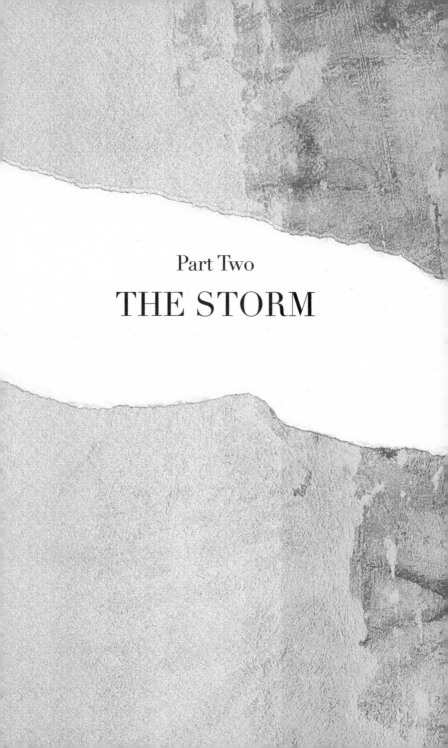

Part Two

THE STORM

1

The wind was driving down now, flat off the sea. A child had left an inflatable ball in the yard beneath the camellia tree. Eva watched it lift and spin, a wet pink smear across the sky, hurled against the wall. It lifted again and she saw it coming, an invisible hand slamming it at her. It struck the window before her and dropped, a bell rolled bleakly inside it. They heard news of the approaching typhoon just after Akiko and Daniel left. Eva frowned with worry, for she felt the spirit of the storm, a malevolent stirring thing upon whose back they must helplessly ride.

Akiko and Daniel had not returned and anxiety tightened in Eva. She dared not think or panic rose. A flurry of rain stung the window, then again retreated. It was almost dark and the iron gate of the orphanage had already sunk into the dusk. In the sphere of light about the porch rain fell solid and hard, like a curtain, then blew wild as the wind caught it. And still she did not hear their returning voices. There was only the hum of wind, and lashing rain. Eva turned from the window, it was almost dinner time.

She let herself out. Immediately the umbrella strained in

her hands, alive, pulling her with it; rain whipped about her. She ran, crossing the road to her own small house. Usually she returned home about this time, but tonight she would not leave the orphanage until after the typhoon. She just had to shutter the house. She let herself in and the dry silent shelter of the place closed about her. She leaned against the door, and the house seemed to reflect her melancholy, and hung like a weight about her.

The rain thrust in, soaking her as she opened the window and pulled out the heavy wooden shutters from their boxes, and slid them into place. Soon it was done, and the house was blind and closed, but panic filled her again. What if Akiko did not return? What if Kyo claimed her? And the girl was glad to go. Akiko. She said the word aloud, and there was numbness now within her. She remembered again how often the child had asked those questions. Who was she? Where is she? My mother? Oh God. Please God. Eva buried her face in her hands as the evening fell thick around her.

Returning to the orphanage, the gate was pulled from her hand by the wind and slammed behind her. The umbrella was all but useless; rain stung her neck. Under the windows of the surgery a bed of tall chrysanthemums dipped and swayed, their yellow heads a mad orchestra in play. The red berries of the elder tree were strewn on the path, smashed and black. Through the lighted frames of the orphanage windows she searched for Akiko's head, but found only Eiko Kubo and Yoshiko Mori dismissing children from the dining room. The rain had eased briefly, but the wind thrashed on in branches and leaves above her, trees tossed against the sky. Soon darkness would come down and seal them in the storm. Eva felt a new fear then, an inexplicable premonition.

She found the younger children gathered in the recreation room, talking excitedly above the bright squares of comics and games. Eiko, Yoshiko and Sister Elaine stood before the television. They turned to Eva.

'The course is unsteady, they say, it could still change,' Yoshiko said excitedly. Eva joined them at the television.

'... the typhoon will hit the Honshu mainland. The Kansai area is already within the outer periphery of the typhoon which is expected to hit Osaka at nine thirty tonight. Evacuation procedures continue in the Tenoji area of Osaka, where the eye of the storm is expected to pass. Typhoon 21, a category 5 superstorm, is one of the most ferocious typhoons recorded in recent years by the Meteorological Agency. Residents of Kansai area are again warned to stay indoors and keep tuned to the weather news ...'

On a satellite photo of the Japanese archipelago the storm track was a bulbous serpentine thing, unmoored and wild above the land. She could see the eye, clear and vacant, in the midst of cloudy hysteria. A man in souwester and galoshes appeared on the screen and stood, microphone in hand, backed by a raging sea. He began to speak with difficulty against the wind. 'Three people were killed near here when a concrete wall collapsed on ...' Eva turned away.

'It's going to be very bad,' said Eiko, 'they say even those side winds will be abnormally strong.'

'There are no shutters to these windows. Can we board them up in any way?' suggested Yoshiko.

'Where will we get wood or board now, the storm is already upon us, as you can see,' Eva said. 'The old building has weathered many typhoons before now.'

'Brown paper tape will strengthen the windows and prevent flying glass. And we have plenty of that,' Sister Elaine remembered.

'Yes, we could do that,' Eva nodded. 'There is a supply in one of the upstairs storerooms. I'm going that way, I'll bring it down.'

It was dark in the corridor, the sound of the television droned on. Eva switched on the light and went upstairs to inspect the two storerooms upstairs. The rooms were due the next week for major repairs; a main beam was rotted. The orphanage, beneath its plaster facade, was a wooden structure, as were most older buildings in Japan and rot was an eternal hazard. But they would not know how bad it was until the workmen came. She had not worried earlier, accepting the periodical treatment and repair implicit in a wooden structure. And there were plans, already under view in Osaka, to expand and entirely rebuild the old home. But in the typhoon the house could ill afford the vulnerability of rot.

She could not tell yet from which way the wind came, whether it skirted the house or blew obliquely at that section with the dormitories above the dining room. She opened the door and found the light had gone, the switch was dead. The room was dark, the branches of a tree thrashed against the glass and thinly sliced draughts cut up at her. The windows were faintly luminous with the last remnants of dusk, the black struts of trees moved outside. It was as she feared. The wind blew off the sea, flat onto the house from the back. She could feel it, for even now the room vibrated gently and creaked, like a ship upon water. And there was the sound of the wind, a low deep whistling round the house.

She stood in the shelter of the door, and did not feel the power of the storm until she crossed to the window. Then the wet branches whipped against the glass again and she stepped back, fearful, for the trees outside, blacker still than the black wild sky, threw themselves wilfully about, writhing like chained animals. Behind the orphanage, the slope of the hill was crowded with pine trees. They moved and moaned and she dared not think the thoughts that came as she recognised the danger. For there is nothing, she thought, there is nothing we can do.

Eva turned quickly away and heard the noise then, like the scratch of a small clawed animal. But it was only the boy, Kenichi, wedged into a corner of the room. His eyes swung between her and the window, terrified. For a moment they observed each other silently as he pressed himself against the wall.

'It is all right,' she said at last, for she felt the unseeable thing that reached out to her from the child. 'You must not be frightened. We are all together. There are others much younger than you. You will have to help them, they must not see you are frightened.'

He looked at her, unblinking, his eyes fixed on those things he could not express. And made no sound, made no move. Eva stood quietly before the child until she was sure her presence reassured him. Stepping forward she touched him on the shoulder, lightly. He did not move, except to turn his frightened eyes to the window once again.

'Will it come?' It was the first time he had spoken. The first time she had heard his voice.

'No. I do not think so. But I am with you, we are all here together. There is nothing for you to fear. It will soon be gone.' She lifted her hand from his shoulder and stroked, just once, as she would a small animal, the rigid curve of his head. Then she turned him gently to the door.

'Come. We will go down now.'

Near the door she collected from a box several rolls of the brown paper tape, and shut the door behind them. Halfway down the stairs she felt him hesitate. He gave a sudden brittle look, pulled away and ran ahead, disappearing into the recreation room. But she knew he could not so easily withdraw now to isolation.

She heard the crash of the front door then and the sound of Daniel's voice.

2

Eva could not ask the question. The words were there, mute in her face, and would not move on her tongue. She stood before Daniel on the last stair, tense and straight. She did not see Akiko.

He watched her, not knowing himself what to say.

'It was bad. Very bad,' he told her quietly at last. 'It was nothing like what she expected. She is in quite a state.'

'Where is she?' Eva asked stiffly, preparing herself.

'I don't know. She disappeared as we came in the door.'

Relief pumped through her then, and beat like a pain in her head.

'You had better change. You're drenched. Here is the key, I have locked up the house. We shall have to stay here tonight.' As she said it she saw in her mind again the creaking mass of trees, blacker than the night.

'Akiko?' Daniel asked, but Eva just nodded. Daniel turned

again to the door.

Sometimes when Akiko was small, she had shut herself away in the the utility room. One time, Eva remembered, had been after a kitten died. It lay behind the kitchens, a small *tatami* matted room they used for ironing that opened onto a yard where they pegged out washing.

She walked through the deserted kitchen and slid open the door. In the darkness beyond the tall-legged bodies of ironing stands, she saw Akiko, crouched upon the narrow, glassed-in veranda. There were tough paper sacks of rice and flour and two obsolete ceramic braziers. Usually a dry dusty smell pervaded and the veranda warmed quickly in a sheltered sun. Now there was just a damp fustiness as rain pounded the roof, loud as falling pebbles. Wind hammered the loose panes of the glass doors, and water dripped in the runners.

'Akiko.' Eva could not hear her own voice above the noise. She manoeuvred her way across the room between the ironing boards and squeezed onto the veranda. Akiko did not move. She sat huddled in a comer, knees drawn up, head buried in her arms. Eva knelt before her, but there was nothing she could say; her feelings were beyond words.

Against Akiko's shoulder the black window shook and streamed, a wall of water. Behind it was the blur of an upstairs light that should have been comforting. But instead, in the watery grave of the window, it swam and slipped and lost all shape. Beside Eva the rim of a ceramic brazier pushed into her hip; she recognised it. Long before it had stood in the kitchen of Eva's house. She had sat with the child before it, resting mugs of hot sweet tea upon its broad blue ledge; inside, the solid core of coals had glowed like a secret cave. Now, covered with dust, it lay unused, a pile of grey ash still locked within it, desolate as the memories to which there is no return. In the wet, pounding darkness Akiko crouched on the veranda, her emotions demolished, no more than a heap of fragments. Eva hurt with a love too physical to express and prayed for the strength to comfort.

'Akiko.'

After a time the girl raised her head. Eva took her in her arms then, and felt the wet of tears on her neck as the wild night closed in upon them.

Eventually, she left Akiko and returned to the main part of the orphanage. The high windows of the corridor rattled as Eva walked quickly by, her mind filled again with images of the black writhing menace of the trees. She glanced at her watch: it was seven-forty. Some decision had to be taken. The wind vibrated deeply now beneath and seemed to charge the house at intervals, attacking viciously.

She found them all in the dining room, taping the windows, and smiled. It resembled the hanging of Christmas decorations. Eiko Kubo stood upon a ladder, Sister Elaine on a table beneath a window. The older children utilised chairs, their lower extremities in the safekeeping of friends, who clung as they stretched to the dark wet windows with long tails of sticky tape.

The room was brightly lit, and the children ran about busily, measuring and dampening the brown paper strips. Emiko and Kimiko appeared to have swaddled themselves together. Yoshiko Mori chided and disentangled. Hiroshi's plaster bore a brown striped pattern. Sister Elaine looked menacingly over her shoulder and issued a futile order as the children ran and laughed. Only Kenichi sat by himself on a solitary chair, and some distance away sat Jiro, a sketchbook on his knee.

Yoshiko Mori stared at the boys, and then walked over to Jiro, bending to speak to him quietly. He picked up his sketchbook and followed her to Kenichi.

'I want two strong boys to lift some tables at the other end of the room,' she said. 'You look like the strong man I need, Kenichi.' The child scowled and looked away.

'Yes. You can't expect to sit there like that. Everyone else is working. Come along.' Eiko Kubo stopped in passing, and spoke out forthrightly as usual. Kenichi growled angrily and shrank back into his chair.

'Ssh,' Yoshiko exclaimed impatiently. 'That is not the way, Eiko, you always say the wrong thing. You don't have to help, Kenichi. I just thought you would be the best one to ask. You look stronger than all of us put together.'

Leading small Toshio by the hand Tami came up to Kenichi. 'We all have to help each other here, I always look after Toshio. Now be a good boy.' She put her head on one side and spoke in a small high coaxing voice as she had heard Yoshiko do.

'Leave him alone,' Eiko Kubo decided and marched firmly off.

'Please, Kenichi,' Yoshiko pleaded.

'Please, Kenichi,' echoed Tami.

'Come on,' said Jiro. 'Afterwards I'll show you my drawings. You can try my new pencil if you like.'

Kenichi looked at him hard, under a brow of thunder. Slowly, he got up and allowed them to lead him away, still glowering.

'What a good boy,' Tami announced patting his belligerent back. She turned to pick up Toshio, and staggering under his weight, hurried after Yoshiko.

Daniel joined Eva at the door where she stood watching. 'Akiko?' he asked.

'She's coming. She's gone to change her wet clothes too.'

'Is she all right?'

'She'll need time.'

Daniel nodded. 'The wind is from the back, I can feel it. Should we not tape the upstairs windows?'

'Yes, take some older children with you. I am worried about the trees, not that we can do much, but they're right in the path of the storm. There have been typhoons before many times, we've weathered through all conditions. But tonight for some reason, I do feel worried, they say these are record strength winds. I think it best the children sleep down here. I don't remember feeling so worried before.'

'Tell me what else I can do,' said Daniel.

'We shall have to bring down mattresses and blankets off the beds.'

Daniel nodded and turned to the dining room as Akiko appeared. Her face was drained, her eyes puffy, but her voice was controlled when Eva explained their circumstances.

'I'll help Daniel see to the beds,' she said quietly. Daniel took her hand and led her into the dining room. Eva stood and watched them thoughtfully, wondered then and hoped.

Eva turned into the kitchen to make some cocoa ready for when the children eventually bedded down. Akiko and Daniel had helped to organise the bringing of mattresses from upstairs. Eva heard the thud of things humped downstairs, and Daniel's voice at intervals instructing the excited children. Eiko and Yoshiko pushed tables to one side of the dining room with the help of Jiro and Kenichi, and arranged the mattresses and blankets as they arrived, helped by the older girls.

Junko whirled suddenly into the kitchen about Eva.

'Look, look. I'm the wind.' She rushed around between the tables. 'Now, I'm a leaf blowing in the sky.' She swung her arms about, excited, and ran out. Silence descended upon the kitchen again as Eva broke hard lumps of cocoa under a spoon.

The rain drove down in sheets upon the window. Wind howled and scuttled about in the darkness outside like a live animal, every so often striking the building brutally, so that it shuddered. Eva stared apprehensively at the window and looked quickly away again. She got out a large saucepan and filled it with milk, and a knocking began at the front door then. An urgent, brassy note, repeated like a cough in the voice of the storm. When Eva pulled open the door wind flung her back, and rain thrust in. Arthur John Wilcox stood before her.

3

Arthur occupied the doorstep, a sodden ghost of his former self. The stiff brim of his hat held water like a moat and dripped before his nose.

'I am forced to ask you, Dr Kraig, to extend a little hospitality to a hapless traveller,' said Arthur Wilcox. 'It is not my wish to intrude, not my wish at all. Rather, something arranged by greater minds. Yes indeed, greater minds, and a little damp in the carburettor too, I think. Deuce of a mess, damn car's stopped dead, only serviced last week, one hundred and twenty thousand yen. Dead as a doornail, and not a jolt from your gate.' He sniffed loudly and pulled himself up. Water trickled from the brim of his hat before his nose, and was at intervals brought into contact with his moustache and tongue. It was of a fresh, pure taste, not unpleasant. He waited for Eva Kraig to invite him in.

'Trouble is, not as young as I was. Forced to admit it at last. In the old days a bit of bad weather would not have deterred. No indeed,' Arthur said as Eva Kraig took his raincoat and spread it across several hooks in the hall. He watched it drip onto the floor, and placed his hat on a peg above.

'Some kind of a blockage a bit further up, branches and soil and rocks and things. The drains are blocked, too, road's running like a river. Have to beware of landslides tonight, expecially on hills like this. You'd better watch out, there is no retaining wall behind you. Nasty predicament you'd be in with a landslide. Mustn't ramble on though, just a bit of respite, and I shall push on. Have to leave the car here, of course.' He sniffed again and stretched his neck in the damp collar of his shirt. He wished he had not been foolhardy enough to go to the club. Instead of looking in the library he had downed two whiskies and fallen asleep in the bar. Eventually the barman woke him to a deserted club, the rain and wind.

'You're much further up the road, Mr Wilcox, and a steep climb at that, and you say too there is a blockage. All this will only get worse, not better. I don't see how you could go on. I suggest you stay with us here, until it's all over,' Eva said firmly, to Arthur's relief. He did not argue the matter, but followed her to the dining room. But the sight within made him hesitate. He had never had close contact with small children, nor professed any liking for them. Now, without defence, he was faced with a roomful of them. He drew back as a few small children ran forward and jumped about Eva, observing Arthur curiously.

'Now, this is Mr Wilcox. He lives just up the hill from us, as some of you may know. His car has stopped near our gate. He is going to spend the typhoon with us.' He heard himself introduced. Many of the other children in the room stopped their industry to survey him. A small boy approached him with a swagger and a broken arm in a plaster cast.

'Why did your car stop? What's the matter with it?' He looked up at Arthur suspiciously.

'A question, I think, of water in the carburettor.' Arthur cleared his throat nervously.

'What's a carburettor?'

'This is Hiroshi, Mr Wilcox.' Eva smiled at the children about her.

'And this is Jun and Takeo and Emiko.' The children stared as Arthur pulled apprehensively at his moustache. He wondered how long the typhoon might last.

'What's a carburettor?' Hiroshi insisted.

'An apparatus mixing air with petrol vapour specifically for the purpose of combustion in the motor engine.'

'What's an apparatus?'

'A mechanical appliance.'

'What's mechanical mean?'

'Now Hiroshi, don't bother Mr Wilcox. He is wet and rather weary, I suspect. Maybe, after the typhoon, Mr Wilcox will show you what a carburettor is.' Eva Kraig smiled blandly. Arthur felt trapped.

'Nobuo and Takeo, find Mr Wilcox a nice comfortable seat.'

'I'm Eiko. Your trousers are wet. Your shoes are wet. We are not allowed to wear wet shoes inside.'

A small girl bounced up to him and pulled at his hand. Arthur looked down, the child seemed a great distance below him. He had never seen anything so tiny so close to him before. She had two thin plaits. His nervousness increased.

'All right, Emiko. When Mr Wilcox sits down he will take off his shoes and socks.'

Arthur turned to Eva in alarm. He saw then that his trouser legs were sodden from the knee down; his shoes left dirty wet stains on the floor. The children clustered around him and Emiko pulled him towards a low canvas chair.

'All the children are sleeping down here tonight, in the dining room, Mr Wilcox. Hence, all the activity. Now make yourself comfortable and give me those wet socks and shoes. I'll dry them off over the stove in the kitchen.' Arthur felt helpless. Reluctantly, he removed his shoes and socks as the children watched with interest and then stared silently at his pale, naked feet on the bare floor, until he felt divested of some private layer of himself.

'Emiko. Fetch Mr Wilcox slippers from the hall cupboard,' Eva ordered, then turned to call a young man to her from the other end of the room. The girl, Akiko, followed him.

'This is my nephew, Daniel. He is visiting us from America,' Eva smiled.

Arthur smiled stiffly too, and nodded to the girl, Akiko. He had watched her grow up, secretly. Kyo's child. Kyo's eyes. But she went off with Daniel again to the other end of the room. Rows of mattresses were being laid out there. Emiko appeared again before him with a pair of slippers.

'Now Mr Wilcox, have you eaten anything? No, I rather thought not. Daniel, Akiko and I have not either, although everyone else has. You'll have a coffee and a sandwich with us. Now make yourself comfortable. You'll have to excuse me.' Eva Kraig turned away. Arthur was left alone with the children. Hiroshi and his plaster cast appeared again.

'What's mechanical mean?'

'To do with a machine.' Arthur looked about him in trepidation. The small bodies of the children surrounded him. A few more came to join the group and stared at him in silence. Their limbs were tiny with the boniness of birds, their heads like dark nodding flowers on frail stems. Rows of eyes observed.

Emiko stepped forward boldly and leaned against his knees, staring up into his face. He marvelled at the perfection of the miniature in her. Hesitantly, she touched his moustache with a finger and drew back quickly.

'Ugh. It's all bristly. What's it for?'

'Err ... err ... decoration,' Arthur replied desperately, knowing the novelty of a moustache in Japan.

'Decoration?' Emiko was incredulous.

'Decoration?' The others echoed and crowded nearer to look.

'Ugh. You have hairs inside your nose,' Emiko announced, completing her scrutiny. Arthur drew back in his chair, but there was not far he could go. The children laughed and ran away, and Arthur was left with Hiroshi.

'What's a carburettor?' Hiroshi continued.

'Go away,' growled Arthur.

At the other end of the room the beds were neatly down. The smaller children, already in pyjamas, clambered in. There was great excitement. Akiko appeared with a tray of hot drinks. Arthur watched her handing round the mugs, bending to each child, settling it in bed.

He had watched the girl grow up. Occasionally even met her with a group of children, coming out or going into the orphanage, when he passed on his evening walk. Sometimes, when she was small she accompanied Eva Kraig on her spasmodic visits to him. She had sat quietly at Eva's side, and gave no sign she recognised the house, although he watched her intently. Perhaps indeed, she did not recognise it. He did not pretend to understand the limit or function of children's memories. Later, as she grew, she appeared sometimes by herself with the dutiful newspapers and bag of fruit or cake Eva sent him. She spoke brightly, but did not stay long. But even then, never once did she give him a sign she remembered him or the house. He saw no flicker in her eyes from the dark, closed box of time. When he thought about it he was relieved, for it had always been a secret. Nobody knew he knew Kyo. His wish to share a memory with the girl was only a wish to return to those moments with the woman. In this secret way he had enjoyed seeing the child grow, enjoyed nobody knowing. He noted those features about the girl that were like her mother, and held them in his mind, like small treasures in a box. With the esoteric pleasure of these thoughts he leaned his head back in the canvas chair, and soon fell asleep.

A knocking sound woke him from a dreamless doze. He sat up and rubbed his eyes. The end of the room where the small children lay was already in darkness. The older children still read in bed under lights in the nearer part of the room. He could not have dozed long: one small child still sat in the dark, finishing its cocoa. He heard the knocking again and the sound of the front door opening. About him the blast of wind and rain lacerated the windows. He was glad he was safe, inside.

Sometimes the wind seemed to run at the building, ramming it head first. Then walls shook and windows trembled with the beating. Outside was the sharp sound of a tin rolling across the concrete yard, rolling and rolling. Arthur was relieved to see, beneath the grey curtains of the dining room, the windows crossed firmly with brown sticky tape. He thought anxiously of his own home, but there was nothing he could do. From the hall Eva Kraig's voice called urgently for Akiko and Daniel. Someone else, it appeared, had come.

He watched the group return to the room with detached interest. The man, Daniel, led the way, carrying the inert body of a woman. Eva Kraig fussed at his side; Akiko trailed some distance behind. Not far from Arthur, Daniel stopped and put the woman down, supporting her as she clung to him. Her wet red hair dripped with rain and was plastered to her head. Eva removed the woman's sodden coat and a pair of spiky red shoes. She pulled a reclining chair forward and they laid the woman on it. She was dressed in a green cocktail dress, as wet as the coat Eva Kraig had removed. There was a cut on her leg, the blood crusted and dark; her stockings were torn and splashed. A slow, wet stain spread beneath her upon the canvas seat of the chair.

In the capacity of interested observer, Arthur got up and walked over. In the chair the woman lay half-conscious; once or twice she groaned. The green of her dress and the deep red of her wet stringy hair were a garish match against her sallow skin. She looked ill, thought Eva, as she poured some precious brandy into a tumbler and pressed it to the woman's lips, supporting her head with an arm. Akiko stood sullenly some distance away, apart from the fussing group. Arthur looked at her curiously, and then back again to the woman, who was now beginning to stir. She opened her eyes, murmured something and struggled forward in the chair.

Arthur started backwards then, half tripping over a mattress. It was as if something had dropped through him, heavy and cold, tearing open the centre of his body. He stared again and recognised the woman, Kyo.

4

Eva closed the door and sat down heavily in the privacy of the surgery. She turned on the reading lamp over her desk. The small travelling flask she had poured Kyo a drink from stood before her, open still. It was kept for emergencies rather than habit, and the present situation was an emergency. Eva poured herself a drink in its cup-like silver cap. She took an ample stinging mouthful and let it course down inside her. Its comfort settled in her belly. There had been no other choice. No choice. The wind nearly blew the woman upon her as she had opened the door. Kyo had staggered and fallen against her, wet, smelling of drink and stale perfume. At first Eva could not believe it.

'How could you have got here in this weather?' It was all she could say in that moment.

'Someone from the bar was driving home, said he lives near here. I took a lift and walked up from the main road. Don't know how we made it, not another car about. Your hill is like a river.' Kyo lurched again against Eva, then leaned back against the wall. 'I kept falling and slipping, I've cut myself all over.' She slid down the wall to sit on the floor. Eva thought her drunk, the smell of liquor was strong about her. She wore a light

cotton raincoat, all wet and muddied, and beneath it a green
lace cocktail dress. Her feet stuck out beneath her awkwardly,
in spiky-heeled red shoes, her ankles were sinewy as a bird's.
She was dishevelled and disreputable. Anger buzzed suddenly in
Eva's head, sharpening her tone as she spoke.

'What do you want? Why have you come? Is it not enough,
all that you have done?' She wanted to open the door and
bundle the wretched woman outside. Yet even as she thought
it, a force of wind struck the door behind her, vibrating through
the walls, reminding her of reality. All she could do was stare
disbelievingly.

'Don't send me away.' Kyo opened her eyes and looked at
Eva. The wet on her cheeks were tears.

'You win,' Kyo said, her voice cracked.

'There was never a battle,' Eva replied with asperity. She
could not believe the woman sat here before her on the floor.

'Why don't you get up?' she asked, more gently. She could
never trust Kyo, she turned from one mood to another, one
stance to another like a chameleon, according to the role of the
moment. How much of this was an act Eva could not tell.

'Kyo.'

'I turned Akiko off. How could I have expected anything
else? Me.'

'Kyo,' Eva said resignedly, for it seemed the woman did not
pretend. For a moment Eva saw in the stroke of an eye and the
line of the brow the essences of Akiko. So that she was reminded
she dealt not with abstractions but human facts. She sighed,
and the hard shape of Kyo dissolved. Sitting there she reflected
nothing but the sad remnants of her own charade. Shabby,
beaten, tawdry remnants. For the moment all her venom and

scheming were gone, anger was futile, Eva saw now. For in the haggard face was only the child she had found in a gutter all those years ago; the same shapes of misery and pain, the same dust of every dream. What chance had there ever been? This fact seemed to connect every expectation. For Kyo illusion would always be reality, and reality illusion. The alternative was unbearable, for life bequeathed Kyo only betrayal after she left Eva.

'I don't know why I came. What shall I do?' Kyo asked, her eyes closed and wet. Mascara was smudged about one eye. She sat motionless against the wall; her head made a wet patch on the plaster. Eva spoke slowly, thinking with each word.

'For the moment what can you do but stay. There is a typhoon all but upon us. That you have arrived is incredible, you certainly cannot return. Afterwards we shall think again.'

'You were always good to me. The only one, ever.' Tears flowed down Kyo's cheeks.

It was all an act; even if there was emotion, the woman was unbalanced. But it distressed Eva all the same as she bent to help Kyo up. 'Come, let's get you warm and dry. Clearly you are most unwell.' Of that at least she was sure now. Kyo nodded, but as she rose she groaned and crumbled to the floor again. It was then Eva called to Daniel and Akiko.

Now she sipped the brandy. Everything is expected, nothing is strange, she thought, and sighed above the cup. The door opened, Akiko came in and took the chair the other side of the desk. Eva sipped her drink and did not speak.

'You'd better have some too,' she said at last. 'We both need it.' She poured a little into a tumbler for the girl. 'Drink it up. That's right. Fortification.'

'She's asleep,' Akiko said. They had persuaded Kyo to

relinquish her wet dress in favour of Eiko Kubo's dressing gown. They had lain her down on a spare mattress and covered her with a sheet.

'Why didn't you tell me more about her?' Akiko said bitterly.

'It would have done you no good to know. You can see that now, can't you?' Eva spoke quietly.

'What will happen?' asked Akiko, almost under her breath. She tipped the tumbler up and drained the brandy.

'Steady on,' said Eva. 'Well for tonight she's here. There's no other way.'

'What does she want?' Akiko questioned.

'I have no idea. Your meeting was bad, she was upset maybe, I don't know. I think she moves as the spirit takes her. Clearly, she is ill, and very unbalanced.'

'She's awful. Awful. I can't believe she's my mother. After all these years of wondering ...'

'I know. I know. But do not hate her. She needs your pity and compassion. Life never gave her a chance. There are many things I shall have to tell you now. But not tonight.'

Akiko said nothing but stared vacantly into the empty glass in her hands. Eva stood up. 'Come. We are needed in the other room.' She reached over and ruffled Akiko's head. 'There is no way, my love, she can claim or harm you. You must not worry.'

Akiko nodded silently and stood up to follow Eva.

It was nine thirty. The children lay on two long lines of mattresses, peaceful, asleep. The dining room was in semi darkness. The adults sat at one end, grouped around a low table, drinking coffee. A light above their chairs was shaded with a towel. Kyo slept on a nearby mattress.

Outside the wind reverberated in a deep sustained boom, like the roll of a distant drum. It seemed to charge suddenly then retreat, only to charge again. A sudden light crash of glass made them start. Daniel got up and went to investigate.

'It's the porch light, something must have blown at it,' he said, coming back into the room. 'I heard tiles rip off the roof too.' He saw while he had been out Eva had placed a hurricane lamp and two torches on the table, in readiness for emergencies.

'I'll go and listen again to the weather news.' Eiko stood up and Yoshiko followed.

'The typhoon was supposed to hit Osaka at nine thirty,' Yoshiko said.

Arthur Wilcox sat up suddenly. 'If that is so, then we must now be, if my geography and storm strategy are rightly remembered, we must now be in the left front quadrant of the storm, or possibly even the left rear quadrant.' Arthur Wilcox frowned with the effort of remembering. 'Yes, it's all coming back.' He turned to Daniel.

'Typhoons, my lad, are spawned at latitudes 10 and 20 either side of the equator, speed at birth six to eight knots, can increase to fifty knots with winds of up to two or three hundred kilometres an hour.' Arthur nodded dourly, pulling down the corners of his mouth. 'Dastardly little things.'

'Where did you learn all that?' laughed Daniel, leaning forward.

'Merchant Navy, young man. Tried it before coming out to Japan. Invalided out, back trouble. Still got it.'

'Did you ever sail in a typhoon, Mr Wilcox?' Eva asked.

'Fortunately, or unfortunately as the case now appears, Dr

Kraig, no. But I learnt my theory. Yes indeed, up here still, fresh as ever.' He pointed to his skull.

'Well, I'm thankful we're here, safe and warm on land. I should not like to be on one of those ships tonight, anchored out in the bay,' Daniel said.

'Not much choice in the matter, young man. Safer than in port, where they might be smashed against a wharf or worse, lifted up and impaled upon pilings.' Arthur dug in his pockets and produced a pen and a scrap of paper. He drew a small circle, then a much larger one about it and divided the whole into four. He pointed to the small circle.

'Here is the eye. These are the four quadrants. Right front quadrant up here most dangerous. Wind in that quadrant blows a vessel to the storm centre. Standard accepted rules, based on Henry Piddington's law of storms devised last century, advise that a sailing vessel in the front quadrant should sail close hauled, or heave to on the starboard tack, so as to proceed away from storm centre.' Arthur announced with a self-conscious cough, and pulled at the corner of his moustache. Not much wrong with the old memory box, he thought. Can't say age is catching up yet. He saw he was observed by all in some wonderment.

'Yes, can't go wrong with old Piddington. Never been bettered yet. Got a copy still on my shelf. Could have done with it down here tonight.'

'Well. I am glad you are with us, Mr Wilcox. We most certainly won't be lost in a storm with you,' Eva laughed. 'More coffee anyone?'

She walked into the kitchen to refill the jug.

5

Akiko watched Arthur Wilcox heating up about his storms. A long bony face and small eyes and between them a great moustache. A muscular, elderly walrus. She looked away in distaste, and stared silently into her coffee. The mug was warm between her palms, its heat an anchor, holding her in the present, not letting her escape. So that she must face the people around her, must accept the reality of what was happening, although it felt like a dream. Her mind bulged painfully with a complexity of detail, yet the simplicity of what had happened hollowed her out. She looked again at the mattress.

Beneath the sheet was a thin huddled shape, a shape that was her mother. Tears pricked in Akiko's eyes. She felt no more than a crumbling of stone, a scattering of ash. It seemed right that outside the wind should scream and lightning split the sky, for she had died. Died for this middle-aged, sallow-skinned woman who was her mother. Who deserved pity and some tears, but not much more.

Akiko, sometimes I like to hope you think of me.
Mother.

Now the words no longer flowered in her head. The images did not bloom but hung like tattered, dirty rags. She had held them silently, expecting beauty, and they had only defiled.

On the mattress Kyo heaved and turned. Her cheek was distorted against a hard bean pillow, her mouth puckered and was pushed slightly open. Eiko Kubo's white candlewick dressing gown gaped to the waist and revealed a narrow sequence of slip and the thin crease of her small flat breasts. The thought ran again in Akiko's head: From the body of this woman I have

been made. And then again, from a long while back came the
words of Mrs Okuno's senile mother, grilling rice cakes on a
brazier. 'I knew her, I did. She would lay with them in the open
if they paid her enough.' She saw now it might indeed be so.
She had forgotten the words, yet they had remained in her head
to parade before her now. In spite of herself she looked again at
the body beneath the sheet, thought of the times it had given
itself, the numerous hands that had run its length and touched
its secret places. She felt nausea in her then, and turned away.
Heat from the coffee mug in her hands claimed her again as she
looked down into its blue well. It showed the reflection of her
own cheek and the ripple of a tear as it mixed with the coffee.

Daniel's hand ran lightly over her back, a caress of silent
support. He watched her, she knew. He was there with her,
beneath the web of social gesture. In a small, bleak way it helped,
like a spot of light at the end of a tunnel. She realised with a
start he was speaking to her, something about the typhoon, and
Arthur Wilcox too was looking straight at her.

'The vertex, young lady, as opposed to the vortex, which is the
eye, is the most Westerly point reached by the centre before the
typhoon recurves to the East. The vertex can also be called the
cod.' She nodded, it was all beyond her. She looked down again
at the mug of coffee, but felt the man's eyes linger upon her.

She did not like him, Arthur Wilcox, who had lived for as
long as she could remember further up on their pine-covered
slope. He resided in the solitary splendour of a ramshackle
house perched on a crag of hill. Two topiary bushes stood either
side of the gate which he proudly and personally trimmed. He
kept to himself, they would hardly have known he was there,
but for Eva's charitable endeavours. She saved her English

subscriptions to newspapers for him, and put aside odd pieces of orphanage fruit, a cake or jar of jam. Once in a while she took them up herself, and sometimes sent Akiko or an older child. For twenty years she had sent Arthur newspapers and fruit. He responded at Christmas with home-made liqueur, and in spring with runner beans from his garden. But no further informalities developed from this stiff gavotte of intercourse.

Akiko remembered when small, sitting with Eva on a patchy green sofa, lowered at one end by a broken frame. She remembered a smell of coldness and a smell of mould, a womanless house of small cheerless rooms, shelves of discoloured books and a golf cup tarnished by the briny air. There was the head of a deer in the hallway upon whose antlers Arthur rested his hat. The eyes of this deer were liquid and bright, a world of the living in the dead, moth-eaten fur of its head. She had clung to Eva's skirt and passed the deer from the further side of Eva's hip. But there was always a strange feeling of residue after she had been to the Wilcox house.

The man's gaze made her uncomfortable, his eyes stayed on her too long, and turned her inside out. But there was something else too, something that rested between the man and the house, that she could never put a finger on. An elusive shadow in her mind. As she grew and sometimes faced Arthur Wilcox alone, the feeling was stronger, not less. She felt his eyes press into her body and search and search her face. As if he asked questions to which he expected no answer. She had deposited Eva's commodities and retreated as fast as she could. But sometimes, turning quickly, the house closed in about her, or echoed strange shadows in her head. There was the feeling of knowing more about the place than what she saw before her.

She felt she knew the graining of floorboards and the crack beneath a door with the familiarity of an ant. Strange elusive ghosts welled up and made her run.

And now across the table, above his scrap of typhoon map, the man looked at her again. His eyes dug into her. A womanless man. Who knew how he interpreted the things he observed. Behind his moustache she glimpsed long thin teeth; his large pale hands were spread over his knees. She moved self-consciously in her chair to curb his stare. He looked at Kyo too, she had not missed that; hungry, furtive looks. She wished she could close the dressing gown that gaped to reveal Kyo's beige satin slip.

But now, as Akiko watched, Kyo stirred, moistened her lips and opened her eyes. She sat up and the bathrobe gaped wider. Lifting both hands to the back of her neck she shook out her damp hair, moving her head in a sinuous way. She took in the group at the table and looked surprised at where she was, then stretched, pushing her arms above her head. Her sleeves fell back on her thin arms as she stifled a yawn and turned her head with a pert little smile. Then, standing up, she walked across to where they all sat.

Akiko stiffened as Kyo came towards her. All the pathos Kyo had arrived with was gone. Akiko saw again in the slim black eyes the customary guile.

6

In the kitchen Eva waited for the coffee to heat. It was silent and deserted, a ghost of its daytime self. The dinner plates were piled unwashed in two large sinks, waiting for the morning cooks and cleaners. The evening shift of staff had not come because of the typhoon. From the dishes came the stale smell of food mixed with the sourness of Arthur Wilcox's drying socks and shoes, spread over a laundry rack before an oil stove.

In the quiet empty room the sound of the storm surged frighteningly. There was a lamp on over the stove; the rest of the room was in darkness. Beyond the windows the moon appeared at times to illuminate great masses of cloud, moving wildly. Eva shivered and turned from the gaping black holes of the curtainless windows. But there was no way to shut out the noise.

Bits of twigs and leaves smacked the windows; sometimes something heavier thudded against the glass and dropped. From beyond the ironing room veranda, where earlier Akiko had crouched, was the repeating noise of a loose corrugated roof in the backyard. Thunk, thunk, thunk, it repeated like a metronome of the storm. In that yard too were six tall metal bottles of propane gas, chained together to the wall. There was no piped gas or water up here, and they had their own well. She could hear a couple of the empty cylinders knocking together, rocked by the wind. The chain that held them together shifted and clunked.

Suddenly, Eva was filled with fear. It seemed outside an inanimate world of solid, immoveable things had been given spirits of their own, and heaved and staggered, like dead creatures brought to life. She turned quickly to a thud at the window, and saw a child's plastic sand bucket roll across and drop. The squashed wet bodies of moths and insects speckled the glass, their torn wings like bits of leaves. In one corner were the mashed green segments of a mantis, like bits of sappy twig, and near it a few yellow petals from a chrysanthemum head. These were the things that not long before had lived and breathed in a rightful world. Now orders were reversed: thick metal feet walked and clunked, roofs moved, stones took flight while birds were smashed to the ground. Something evil was about, something wild and screeching, like a harpie, plunging and swinging above the earth. She remembered again the black thrashing trees, she remembered her fear at the orphanage gate, of the night that would descend and seal them in the storm. A strange, living, shimmering fear.

Her heart beat in her throat then, and she reached for the kettle at its first lusty song, poured it on the coffee grains, and breathed in their bitter, comforting smell. A smell that was reality. Calmer then, she picked up the jug to leave the kitchen.

It was a great tearing ripping sound, a terrible thrashing and groaning, like some giant winged creature struggling free. And then the splintering and a crash that shook the floor in the kitchen.

Daniel, Akiko, Arthur and Sister Elaine came running from the dining room. Eva stood still, coffee pot in hand.

'What is it?' they asked breathlessly.

'It's from the ironing room.' Eva put down the jug as Daniel slid open the ironing room door. A blast of cold wind and rain rushed in at them. Daniel switched on a light in the room.

'It's the backyard roof, ripped clean off and blown into the window.' Wind roared in like a great open-mouthed tunnel, rain sprayed and swirled about them. Over Daniel's shoulder Eva glimpsed the jumbled mound of ironing stands: bodies askew, legs collapsed or stuck up in the air. The white corrugations of the plastic roof poked through the shattered window.

'The room will be ruined. What can we do?' Eva thought of the rain on the matted *tatami* floor.

'Have you anything to board it up with, cardboard, wood?' Arthur inquired.

'No bits and pieces will stand against that wind. Have you no more sliding doors like this?' Daniel pointed to the sliding detachable *fusuma* doors in the ironing room.

'Upstairs, between the two smaller dormitories,' Eva replied.

Daniel and Arthur came back, lugging the two segments of the door. They humped them over the fallen ironing boards and wedged them at an angle against the broken windows. The noise of the storm was forced outside again and they crunched back across the glass carpeting the matting, shutting the door behind them.

As they wiped the wet rain from themselves with towels Eva gave them, the sound of feet beat down the corridor. There was the voice of Eiko and behind her Yoshiko. They burst into the kitchen, excited.

'It's coming here to Kobe. Here. Oh, what shall we do?' They laughed and clung together.

'The typhoon, here to Kobe?' Eva echoed.

'They say it has slowed a little and changed course. It will hit Kobe in an hour,' they cried again together.

On the television this information was continued.

' ... Typhoon 21 leaving a trail of devastation in the wake of its torrential rains and record-breaking winds, dropped speed during the last hour and has changed to a more northerly direction. It is now expected to hit Kobe at ten o'clock tonight. Still retaining a central barometric reading of 968 millibars, Typhoon 21 is speeding forward at the pace of ninety kilometres an hour. Havoc wrought by the storm is expected to extend to thirty eight prefectures in Japan. So far already thirty people have been killed with forty missing and another one hundred and fifty-eight injured. Flooded houses so far number more than eight thousand, roads have been damaged at more than two hundred and fifty places and landslides reported at two hundred and ninety five points. Residents of Kobe are asked to take shelter in substantial buildings. The sudden change of course makes the precautionary measurements of evacuation impossible ...'

They stood in silence until it was finished.

'What shall we do? Oh what shall we do?' Eiko and Yoshiko cried in unified terror.

'Not much choice in the matter, I fear,' Arthur replied. He moved anxiously up and down on the balls of his feet, stretching his neck this way and that. 'No doubt we shall now experience the right front quadrant of the storm, young man. Have to heave to on the starboard tack,' Arthur said to Daniel with a sudden salute of his hand.

But Eva stood still, a coldness suddenly in her body. And she remembered again the fear she had felt in the kitchen and at the orphanage gate.

7

The children slept. In the stillness were small sounds of breathing and an occasional cough. Outside, the wind hammered and raged, rain slapped windows in hard straight sheets. The grey curtains were drawn in the dining room. There was nothing to see, only the noise and an odd shudder through the house.

Arthur Wilcox frequently consulted his watch, and stared into space before him, waiting, a newspaper lay open on his knees. Alternately he picked it up and put it down and looked at his watch. Eiko and Yoshiko giggled over a ludo board and turned for advice to Sister Elaine, who embroidered a sampler beside them. Eva read, Akiko and Daniel spoke quietly together, their chairs drawn apart from the group. Only Kyo yawned and shifted, sipping coffee, drawing on a cigarette in sharp drags. The dressing gown opened on her slim crossed legs and satin slip. She jiggled a foot impatiently and blew smoke, staring at Eva and Akiko.

She did not recognise Arthur. He could see that clearly. Her eyes ran over him blankly, and turned away; for it was twenty years. He was still shocked, still felt the woman a hallucination that would suddenly disappear. But she did not, so that slowly he stared at her for longer intervals from the raised safety of the newspaper. She had changed and aged, and yet she had not. When he looked at her the same excitement twisted in his body, dissolving the years. He tried to define the changes. The red, curling hair had been sttraight and black before. Fine and soft in his hand, like a curtain over his face. He still remembered light from a window, iridescent and prismed through her hair, and the curve of her naked shoulder. Kyo. His heart flickered in his throat. But where were the changes of these twenty years, the furtherance of age? He saw only the same slim body and limbs, the features as before. Age was something buried, a hardening beneath the eyes, a calculation of sallow skin. She looked ill. Not just the ochre tint, but a deadness of her very flesh, sucked bloodless and limp. She coughed in a rusty way as if her throat was scoured with wire mesh. She was a bony, featherless little bird, she was a piece of limp thrashed rag. She was everything that was at an end, well used and cast aside. Kyo. Had she ever been more than this? Yet he still could not look at her without a tightness in his limbs.

She had only used him, he had meant nothing to her. Yet he was grateful, for she did not know what she gave. She did not know the shadows and confines of his life. Unaware, she tossed them aside and the light had dazzled him. Dazzled. Lit him up from within, so that he had existed only for the moments when she came. Kyo.

He remembered the first time. She had brought the eternal newspapers from Eva Kraig on two occasions before. He had not been long in the house then, barely knew of Eva Kraig, and appreciated her thoughtful gesture. Twice the girl had come instead of Eva. She worked in the orphanage, she said. Her eyes had travelled the room, travelled over him, lazy, calculating eyes. That third time she did not turn to go, but instead wandered round, looking, touching.

'What's this?' she said, before the photo of him as a child with elder brothers and parents. He stepped forward to explain, standing close to her. He did not finish speaking before she turned, unbuttoning slowly the tight white blouse, button by button by button, watching him all the time. He backed away, his whole body contracting, for how could he tell her of his fear. Of the disease that became the madness that killed his philandering father. Of his mother's embittered recriminations that tied him in guilt-ridden, inexplicable knots, that impeded his very life. He backed away, trembling, until there was only the wall behind him. Then she had taken his hand and placed it beneath the blouse.

She came regularly then, whenever she could, for an hour, sometimes two, barely longer. She said it was enough, although to him a day would have been no more than an hour. Kyo. Her body gave him life. Gradually he relaxed, for nothing seemed to happen to him that was not whole and good. Beneath him she throbbed. 'I can't live without it,' she whispered once. 'I can't live like she does at that orphanage. She wants nothing for me but good, I know. But she could never understand the kind of woman I am.'

The kind of woman I am. He remembered the words, and he knew then the distance he always sensed. He could have been anyone for her, as long as he was a man. But it made no difference to the burning within him.

Then she went away, placed by Eva Kraig with an American family on a military base. He thought he would never see her again. It was two years before he did. Then she came with the child, and stood on his doorstep. It had been a night like this, of wind and rain. Her clothes and hair were wet.

'There was nowhere else to go,' she said.

It had taken him some time to comprehend the child, to realise it was hers and nothing to do with the orphanage. Akiko, she said. Her name was Akiko. She jiggled the small creature in her arms and told him about that bastard, Joe; her English had improved.

He lit a fire because she shivered, peeled off her wet clothes himself and wrapped her in a blanket, and his body warmed again. He carried her to the bedroom, shutting the door upon the child. But through the wind and rain and Kyo's body he heard its cries and the sound of small fists, desperate on the door. He had got up, angry, shouted and shut the door again.

Kyo laughed and drew him down. Almost at once there were the cries again and the pounding on the door. Afterwards he had turned away in distaste at the child's wet and swollen face, at the slime that ran from her nose to her mouth, and the choking sobs even Kyo could not stop. He turned away, he knew nothing of children.

She stayed three days, and he did not even ask her why. She cooked and lay warm beside him. He did not go to work. Yet only at night, when the child slept, were they free of its frettings, of its small hands upon the door. Kyo found a worn sock of Arthur's, stuffed it with remnants of a withered cushion and embellished it with button eyes and lips of rough chain stitch. But still the child would not be quiet, its fists hammered through his dreams, until she left it at the orphanage.

'That's why I came,' she said, incredulously. 'I'm going to Bangkok, to a cabaret opening there. I can do nothing with a child.' She shrugged, and found a box that had held some onions, and lined it with a cloth. Later that night she placed the sleeping child in it with some clothes and the button-eyed sock. She carried it down herself, she would not let him help.

'Eva took her in. I waited behind a bush. I saw,' she reported upon return. Holding out a hand she drew him near, a strange, wild look in her eyes. She might have deposited a box of fruit on the orphanage doorstep.

That night was long and quiet, and in the morning she was gone. On his desk she left the small blue vase with a tag about it, 'To Arthur'. He never saw her again, until she came here tonight. Twenty years.

There must be a way to make her see it was him, some way to attract her attention. Nobody had introduced them. He looked at her hard and spoke up loudly.

'I wonder what our bearing is of the centre in this storm.' Kyo looked at him without interest.

'How could you determine that, Mr Wilcox?' Daniel asked.

Arthur kept his eyes on Kyo, but she gave no sign at the sound of his name. She looked back at Akiko, and puffed out a quantity of luxuriant smoke. He spoke loudly again, to catch her eye. 'Buys Ballot's law.' Arthur dug in his pockets for a compass. 'Dashed useful little things, always carry one with me. Now, according to Buys Ballot's law, we face the wind. If it veers to the right we are in the right semicircle, and the other way we are in the left. A non-shifting wind indicates we are in the storm track, either ahead or behind the centre.' Arthur spoke earnestly, sitting forward in his chair. Kyo met his eyes and held them for a moment.

It was no use, she did not recognise him. It hurt, for to him each moment all those years ago, although no longer totally recallable, still released a warmth into him. Kyo. He would not remind her, he had his pride. Instead he observed her sadly and lowered his eyes. And then, from outside, without a warning, the typhoon came down upon them at last.

8

It was like the smashing of a vial of wrath. Swift and hard, unmistakable. It exploded around the house. The beams, the glass, the floor shook under the avalanche from above, like an earthquake in the storm.

Eva started from her chair. Oh God, she thought. Oh God.

The children woke and began to scream, until they were all astir, clustering round the adults, the little ones hugging worn stuffed toys.

'We must keep calm,' said Eva. 'Put your dressing gowns on and sit together at this end of the room.'

They must all be prepared, although she knew not for what. In all the years in Japan, through typhoons that came and went, she had never experienced a direct hit. She did not know what to expect.

'It is only wind and rain. We must keep that in mind, nothing more. And we are safer here together, inside,' she reassured. But her last words were lost in a clap of appalling noise, thunder, wind or a falling building, she did not know what. It was as if the wind tunnelled under the orphanage now, and shook until it shuddered and creaked. Some little ones screamed and clung to her.

'It's only the wind,' she calmed, and turned to Arthur Wilcox. 'How long could this go on?'

'It's barely started. Great variations. Impossible to say. Some storms can be one thousand miles, with a belt like this, five to sixty-five miles, spiralling into the centre. Impossible to say,' he said.

'How about the television?' Daniel asked. 'Or the radio?'

Eiko rushed in that direction and at once rushed back again.

'Just a lot of crackle.'

'Not surprised,' said Arthur.

They fell silent as wind rammed the orphanage in a solid body, coming in wave after shrieking wave. The building vibrated like a fragile box. They stood together, children close about the adults, feeling the vengeance of the storm. The light above them, shaded with a towel, shifted uneasily, quivering. Listening, each saw in their minds the churning sky beyond the roof, lurching, rolling, pitching. A sea of venom, heaving up and thrashing down upon them, again and again. They were frail as reeds or flotsam on the tide. Each felt that passage of darkness in themselves, and the thin white rim of fear.

The wind was many-voiced now, a whole texture of knitted sounds. Of shrieks and wails, of wild drums and the symbols of concussion, a great vicious orchestra in play. A taut thread of tension drew them together. Eva rubbed her hands over the small heads and backs about her, over the nobble of bone and the soft plush of hair. These were her worry now, the children, and quickly then she began to organise the books to be read, and a game to be played to the twirling of a rope. Only action would relax.

> *At one time Hanako's*
> *Tears poured down*
> *Poured down,*
> *Too many tears,*
> *Too many tears ...*

The children's voices began hesitantly to pick up strength. The beat of the rope smacked the floor, the small pounding feet threaded between. The rhythm accompanied the storm, the floor shook gently, on the table coffee cups rattled and the children began to relax. Yoshiko Mori and Sister Elaine twirled the rope, calling names. Akiko began to read to a group of older children. Eiko Kubo went into the kitchen to prepare hot orange juice. Eva turned to Daniel.

'I want you to come with me.'

There was a chill in the upstairs corridor. Draughts shrilled through chinks of the old wooden building. Rain lashed like skeins of leather twine against the windows. She had to raise her voice to speak.

'You must see, you must tell me. They frighten me.' She opened the door of the room for him to see the trees, as earlier she had seen them. But it was dark now. There was little to be found in the matt black world of the windows. The dusk that earlier illuminated the trees was long dead. In the inkiness only the howl of the storm pressed in about them, wrestling the paltry defence of walls. The trees were lost in blackness, their suffering spasms and groans surfaced sometimes through the wind. The limbs of the willows still whipped the glass in a frenzy of self-flagellation. Eva walked behind Daniel to the window and placed a hand on its polished black surface. The glass trembled coldly under her hand, like a shuddering naked body. Outside the night tore and boiled. She drew back quickly, afraid, but Daniel pressed his face to the glass, cupping it in his hands.

'I can't see anything. It's black as hell out there. Not a lamp about.'

Immediately then, lightning struck, as if obeying his request. It sliced the belly of the sky, ripping open its black night flesh, so that in a single lighted frame they glimpsed the slope of trees. Involuntarily Eva reached out and gripped Daniel's arm. They both saw it.

Like a great hand of gnarled fingers thrust up from the earth, the loose roots of a tree were exposed. And the tree itself leaned and lurched like a drunken creature anchored by chained feet.

'Only yards away, one of the first ring of trees. It'll come right down upon us here. There is rot in the main beams, too,' Eva told Daniel.

'The children are in the dining room just under us here. If that tree were to come down on this room ...' Eva worried.

'I'm sure I saw a flattened area in that copse further up, as if smaller trees had fallen, a landslide maybe, the slope is steep.

'Arthur Wilcox said the road was running like a river. There are many mountain streams in this area, the drains that carry them down the hill always overflow in weather like this. We've had small landslides before, but it's the trees that worry me.'

Even as Eva spoke they heard through the wind a creaking wrench of sound. Eva stepped back, hand to throat, waiting. Then the lightning came again, the tree was still there, at a crazier slant.

'Quick, we must get them out of the dining room. It will fall right on this room,' Daniel shouted.

'Get them into the recreation room, in the other wing,' Eva yelled, running behind him down the stairs.

Before they reached the bottom there was a crash of glass and screams and voices. But it was only a window in the dining room, hit by a windblown object. Glass, loose dirt and leaves showered the floor. The wind rushed in, flinging curtains to the ceiling, flapping them wildly like great grey wings. Large slices of broken glass, held by sinews of brown tape, hung loosely, moving in the gale. The wind snaked about, lifting the hair of frightened children, moving skirts, brushing papers from the table, parting and blowing them across the floor. The children huddled against a wall behind Akiko and Sister Elaine. The little ones clung to each other, whimpering, while older ones looked on in agitation and excitement.

'Some thick newspaper,' Arthur shouted to Eiko, who

rushed to the kitchen. He grabbed the nearest two boys, Jiro and Kenichi.

'Get the brown tape,' he ordered, as Daniel and Eva appeared.

'The trees,' Daniel said as calmly as he could. 'The storm has uprooted a tree. It may fall over this room.'

'Come, everyone, to the recreation room. Quickly.' Eva ordered them out. The children hurried to her in the corridor, their voices and bodies throbbed about her in excitement and anxiety.

'Will we stay up all night?' Takeo, Nobuo, and Jun began at once to ask questions.

'Will the tree really fall?'

'What happens to the birds in it then?'

'They fly away, stupid ...'

' ... or get killed.'

'Can we have more orange juice?' Kimiko interrupted.

'Will we get killed if the tree falls?' Emiko demanded.

'And can we have biscuits, too?' Kimiko added.

'How will we live here if the tree breaks the roof?'

'Quiet. Quiet.' Eva put her hands over the ears. 'No questions, just run along quickly.' She patted Hiroshi's fat behind and shook Emiko's plaits. The children jumped in excitement.

'Mariko, take Ruriko.' Eva gave the older girl the small blind waiting hand. Akiko and Sister Elaine hurried the children forward. There was a holiday mood, and some children began to sing as Junko started dancing again.

'I'm the wind, blowing down the house.' She pirouetted about. But Toshio stood terrified, apart from the children, fear holding him taut. Yoshiko Mori scooped him up and soothed him. Tami pulled at her skirt.

'I'll look after him.'

'Do you want to go with Tami?' Yoshiko asked. The child nodded and she put him down. Tami led him away, bending to him maternally.

Eva turned into the dining room. At the far end Daniel and Eiko Kubo stacked mattresses in a pile while Jiro and Kenichi finished patching the window with Arthur Wilcox. She saw Jiro speak to Kenichi in his gentle way, and Kenichi listened without his accustomed belligerence. At least there seemed progress there. The responsibility of mending the window gave him a chance to change his stance. But there was no time to consider Kenichi.

'Come along, quickly. That tree could come down any moment,' she ordered, but the words seemed unreal in her mouth as she said them in the empty solid room. She tried not to think about the tree and what might happen if it fell. The darkness was convulsed outside, a world she did not know.

9

The room was a dim landscape of sleeping shapes, closed and stuffy. The children turned restlessly and threw off their covers. They were squeezed onto the *tatami*-matted floor; the room barely accommodated them all. Nothing had happened, it had been well over an hour.

Eva shifted position, her legs cramped from sitting on the floor. Beside her, Ruriko slept, head on a cushion. Eiko and Yoshiko played cards with Daniel and Akiko. Kyo, Sister Elaine and Arthur Wilcox dozed upright against the walls. Arthur snored gently, a long end of moustache lifting with his breath.

Perhaps nothing would happen, thought Eva. Perhaps she had hustled them into an uncomfortable night in this room for no reason. Outside, the gale hammered on, swelling and tossing. Was there nowhere to escape it, she wondered. Would it ever end?

Beside her, Ruriko stirred and sat up. 'I want a drink. I want the bathroom.'

'Come.' She guided the child from the room towards the bathroom.

'I want orange juice,' said Ruriko. 'Please.' From where she sat on the toilet she wiggled her knees demurely in the confines of her lowered pants.

'Only as it's a special night,' Eva agreed. 'Now, just wait there.'

She crossed the dining room to the kitchen and stood at the door, listening to the laceration of the wind outside, and the shudder of the walls. The dark warren of rooms and passages stretching out above and around her seemed to echo her own tension. The spirit of the storm had turned malevolently upon them and closed around them now.

Her heart began to palpitate and she turned into the kitchen quickly. There the storm beyond the windows seemed about to enter the room, and when she put on the light, the glass reflected images that threw her back upon herself. The gleams of pots and ladles and the bare working surfaces of tables took on a sinister tone.

She leaned against the door and shut her eyes, trying to calm herself. Then she forced herself to straighten, walk across the room, and make a cup of orange juice. She replaced the bottle on a shelf and heard Ruriko's whimper. The child had got herself off the toilet and had come by herself as far as the dining room door.

'Wait there. I'm coming.' Eva saw the child through the kitchen hatch smile at the sound of her voice, reassured. Stretching out her hands, she set off across the dining room.

'Wait,' Eva called again.

Then it happened, like a bolt of thunder from above, as if the sky was ripped apart, a massive retort, shaking the bones from the flesh of the house. Then a terrible tearing and grating, the house shuddering like an earthquake. Great cracks shot across the ceiling of the dining room, opening and widening. Plaster began to drop in clumps from above, the lamp swung wildly. Ruriko screamed, standing blind and tiny in the midst of the room, covered white by a shower of plaster dust.

Eva ran, snatched the child up, dived under a table and crouched there. For a moment she thought it over, but the wrenching and tearing began again. A great splitting and grinding racked the building, as if it doubled up like a house of cards, folding and falling in upon itself. It seemed the sky came down above her. Chunks of plaster fell thudding on the table top, the dust rose up in clouds, coating her face and mouth. The room was in blackness. She clutched the child to her, shielding it with her body. They clung to each other until it was over and there was only the bawl of the wind again. And waited some more. But nothing came. Then Eva crawled out from beneath the table.

They came running from the other room then, crunching over the debris, encircling her, leading her out. Someone took the child from her arms, her mouth was dry and thick with dust. The voices were confused about her, she was conscious of shadows, swinging rhythmically over the walls behind the beam of torches. The rubble on the floor reminded her strangely of the crumble of icing from a demolished birthday cake. Looking up she saw a huge yawning wound split the ceiling. Within it, the dark wet trunk of the tree swelled out obscenely. The rain dripped through about it, and formed puddles on the floor. They led her back to the other room.

Daniel sat her in a chair. From a flask Eiko filled a cup with warm Japanese tea, and pressed it into her hands. The children were astir again within the room. There seemed nothing but bodies and voices, she wished she could push them all away.

'I'm all right. All right,' she kept repeating. In a corner she saw Ruriko crying upon Yoshiko's lap. On the wall, a clock stared over their heads, beating on, indifferently, in the room.

10

Afterwards, of the next few moments she remembered only the sound of that clock, and the sight of Daniel's grey suede moccasins, implanted firmly by her chair. She remembered a tear in the seam of the shoe, she remembered thinking to remind him to have it repaired.

Then the world blew up about them. Another tree fell, not upon the house, but across the back yard, smashing down on to the bottles of propane gas, exploding a cylinder there. But this they knew only later. At that time there was again just the sickening grind and split of wood, the floundering noise of the tortured trees, in that breaking dying moment. Hearing it Eva felt a sudden calm take hold of her as she gave herself up to whatever fate awaited them all. The spell of the storm was upon them; there could be no escape.

The savagery of the blast of the exploding gas cylinder threw them to the floor. All at one moment, in a great wave of sound, was an eruption of glass and plaster and wood. Something seemed to pulverise the room, and left it in a second, maimed and mauled.

She thought they must be dead, and dared not raise her head from her arms. Before her the room resembled the desecration of a battlefield, with limp strewn bodies and a residue of rubble. Wind and wet lashed in like scavengers through the torn-out windows, stirring dust and mixing mud with splintered wood. But miraculously they began to stir, one by one uncurling, standing, moving limbs testily, brushing off grit and dust.

The wind foamed, spraying the room as it blustered through the shattered windows and staggered about. Beneath its racket the children began to whimper in the dark demolished room. Eva reached for the torch, and flicked it on. Its scanty beam passed over the room, throwing up ragged facets of disorder, the stricken dusty faces of children, an arm, an ear, a blooded hand, Hiroshi's cast with its playful brown paper lattice, a crimson stain on Sister Elaine's white habit, the powder of dust on Arthur's moustache. The noise of the wind howled on about them.

'Is anybody hurt?' Eva called into the darkness.

To her great relief, there were no more than minor cuts and bruises, and only Yukio bled badly from some flying glass. Arthur produced a pencil torch and guided Yoshiko by its delicate wand in search of the first aid box.

The shock began to subside, fear seeped back into the

children. They unleashed words and sobs all at once, and surged towards Eva's one small light. There was the crush and crumble of glass and dust, and a loud cry again from an injured child.

'Just stand quite still until we find some torches,' Eva ordered. When Arthur and Yoshiko returned with the first aid box, she left the room with Daniel.

In the corridor, chill and wind consumed the building, thrusting in through great ripped vents. It lifted Eva's skirt and the loose hairs at her neck, slapping wetly about her face.

'It's like the Blitz,' she said, swinging the torch about. The dust whipped up by the wind settled thickly on her lips. 'What could it have been? What could have caused this?'

'Give me the torch.' Daniel walked to a shattered window.

'It's the gas cylinders. Another tree has fallen across the backyard, onto those bottles. I can see them. One must have exploded.' Daniel swung the torch from the window. There was a thick dense smell of smouldering wood.

'Is there fire?' Eva asked, alarmed.

'There doesn't seem to be. Probably the rain squelched it.'

'It's a miracle nobody's hurt,' Daniel said, coming back.

'Only because we are in the other side of the house. If we had been in the dining room ...' Eva could not finish.

'We have three more great torches, two in the kitchen and one in the surgery.' Eva put her mind to the present. She led the way, stepping over a litter. A great shard of wood swung from the dining room door and Daniel pulled her quickly back. Inside the room, every window had been blasted out.

'It's like a bomb has dropped,' Eva said again, unable to move from the metaphor, there was no other way to describe the havoc. The gale snaked and whined through it all, so that in her mind Eva saw the wrecked building like some ruined, windy catacomb, and shivered.

In the kitchen a part of the wall had collapsed. The room blended at last with the savage night that howled and lashed, insatiable. Pots and bowls and smashed chinaware were strewn amongst the rubble, and Arthur Wilcox's sock hung limply from a splintered cupboard. Plaster and brick and struts of wood mixed with the contents of the garbage bucket, blasted over the room. A ladle still swung from its hook in the wind and knocked against a tiled wall. Wire poked from crumbled plaster.

'Oh God,' Eva gasped and hid her eyes.

Daniel stepped carefully over the mess, to the drawers where the torches were kept. Eva waited in the doorway, shielding her face from the wind and flying grit. They went next to the surgery and here the damage was minor. Except for one cracked window the room still stood intact.

'We must get them in here. We must think what to do. Oh God,' said Eva. And again. 'Oh God.'

They returned to the children, the torches flaring out before them, great searchlights opening up the night. Now they could see the recreation room was a total disaster. Cracks patterned the walls, the ceiling bulged dangerously above them, still unable to decide its fate. Every so often it creaked and offered up a shower of dust. The children quivered in fear, their limbs patched with first-aid plasters.

'Yukio is bleeding badly. We've done the best we can. But I've already had to change his dressing once. Mariko is a bit concussed, something fell on her, but I think she's all right. Apart from them it's just minor cuts. It's unbelievable, considering,' Akiko told Eva.

Daniel returned from another reconnoitre. 'It's all charred at the back. I can see it from the window. There must have been a great flare of fire we didn't see from here. But it didn't last long in that rain, thank God.'

'We must get out of here, it's an utter mess. The surgery is in better shape. We've water and towels there, we can clean up the children,' Eva told the women. The light of the torches reassured the frightened children and they began to file from the demolished room. Eva waited by the door, counting them out, calming where she could.

There were the last few children in the room, Arthur, Kyo and herself, clustered round the door. The middle of the room was empty. Eva turned flashing her torch about the room. In its beam she saw the ceiling opening slowly in a black wound, as a net of balloons might open over the heads of merrymakers. The ceiling gaped and emptied suddenly down upon them, innards overflowing in a spew of solid matter and a cloud of dust.

Arthur Wilcox flung himself protectively upon Kyo, pressing her before him to the wall. Eva pushed the children through the door and crouched against the frame, her hands shielding the top of her head. The wind flung itself about in unbridled flurry. She pressed her arms to her ears as a final vomit of plaster and splintered wood collapsed in one huge belch upon them.

A shroud of dust enveloped her and debris showered upon her head. Her nose was filled with fine, thick silt; she could not breathe and sank down on her knees, a great sob bursting within her.

'God. Please help us. Help us.' She choked upon the words, and suddenly then was aware of silence. Silence. She took her arms from her head and lifted her face. There was a low, strange mewl of wind, which died suddenly and stopped. Then nothing. Nothing.

Slowly, she got to her feet. In her mind was the scene of a biblical miracle she had seen in a film long ago. She saw again the shape of God in technicolour, and a monstrous parting of the waves.

In the silence was only the light sift of dust as it still trickled from the ceiling, and a fall of grit from her skirt. Arthur stepped back and Kyo unfolded from beneath him, looking about in wonderment.

'It's God's own miracle. Nothing less,' Eva whispered hoarsely. 'It's over. Thank God. Over.' Relief filled her.

Arthur bent his head and waggled a finger in his ear, dislodging a plug of dust. He brushed the dirt from his moustache and cleared his throat.

'The worst, Dr Kraig, is yet to come. This is merely the eye.'

11

'The eye. The eye of the typhoon,' breathed Eva. She remembered the satellite photo on the television, and the black hole of the eye: a sinister, vacant thing. In the strange sudden silence she leaned against the door, and let the stillness wash through her. Arthur Wilcox cleared his throat again. Beneath his foot a sod of plaster grated and collapsed.

'According to the books, the worst is yet to come,' he repeated.

'The worst yet to come? Oh surely ... no ...' Eva echoed disbelievingly.

'If we were now to look at a barometer, we should see the lowest reading of our lives,' Arthur informed her.

Daniel appeared suddenly before them. 'It seems to be over, at last.' He smiled, brushing dirt from his sleeve.

'Just the eye, lad, the eye.' Arthur shook his head.

'And the worst, according to Mr Wilcox, is yet to come,' Eva said quietly. Her mind was beginning to work again.

'Jesus,' Daniel exclaimed, and repeated the word as he saw the fallen ceiling behind them.

'We must bear in mind the winds are rotating. Therefore they will reappear now from the opposite direction, and stronger,' Arthur said.

'What are we to do?' Eva twisted her head anxiously.

'There'll be nothing left of the house ...' Daniel said, horrified. 'Those trees are like loose teeth, so much top soil has been washed away. There have been landslides, I could see it with the torch. There is mud all piled up at the back of the house. More trees could fall.'

'We must leave,' Arthur decided. 'We must evacuate without delay.'

'How long do we have?' Daniel asked.

'Where can we go?' Eva demanded.

'We have maybe twenty or thirty minutes at the most. It varies, but not more. We must go to the nearest solid structure. We must go to the Coopers,' Arthur announced.

'The Coopers? That house on the beach?' asked Daniel.

'They are on the sea, is it safe?' said Eva.

'That house is a ferroconcrete fortress, there is nothing it will not withstand. It is the nearest house. We shall be much safer there than here. If we hurry we can just do it. There is not a moment to waste. Hurry,' Arthur said.

'Come along now. *Come along*,' he ordered, propelling them from the room, his voice rising desperately. 'Try the phone, young man, let them know we are coming. Maybe they can send some help,' he suggested to Daniel. In the torchlight he danced on his toes in great agitation.

'The phone is dead,' Daniel shouted from the hall.

'Quick. Get the children out. All keep together. We must be quick, or we shall be caught on the road in that backlash. It'll be vicious, just vicious when it starts again.' Arthur jigged about, gesturing with his arms. A great wave of feeling filled him, he saw himself already at the head of the orphanage battalion.

From the open door of the surgery the children stared in terror, the smaller ones crying. Kimiko's voice rose hysterically as Yoshiko Mori tried to calm her. Akiko and Eiko appeared with armfuls of clothes.

'We dashed up to get these, the children will need them, they've only pyjamas on. It's such a mess up there. We could only get to the small dormitory, the tree has smashed in right through the corridor. That rot must have made it all so brittle. This is all we could manage to get.' Akiko spoke breathlessly.

'Kimiko, Kimiko. Here is your rabbit.' Eiko Kubo waved a toy at the crying child.

'We have to get out of here,' Eva said desperately.

'And quickly,' Daniel added. 'The calm of the eye won't last long.'

'Get some things on the children,' Akiko said to Eiko.

They began to pull clothes on the children, regardless of size. Small Toshio stood rigid with fear, unable to cry or move. Tami bent to him.

'We'll be all right, Toshio. I don't think we will die. What a good boy you are.' She buttoned him into the jersey Yoshiko gave her.

'Put your arm in here, Toshio.' But the child could not move. A puddle formed about his feet.

'What a time to wet yourself,' Tami exclaimed and gave him a sudden smack.

'Tami. No.' Yoshiko took charge of the child.

Emiko tearfully nursed her arm, embellished with first-aid plasters. Kimiko sucked her thumb, quiet now, hugging the rabbit. Junko strained to be gone, hovering on her toes. No jersey could be found to accommodate Hiroshi's plaster cast, so they wrapped a blanket around him.

Arthur Wilcox strode manfully about, as the children were clothed and organised.

'Enough. Come on. There is no more time. They'll have to go as they are.' With Daniel's help he herded the children into a rough file.

'Quickly. Quickly. Get those children outside. We've fifteen minutes at the most.' He snapped out his orders through a dusty moustache. Movement began about him.

12

There was no wind, not a breath. The air was motionless. They paused outside the gate, taking deep breaths of freshness. It was not completely dark. On the horizon of the bay a great white bank of clouds rose up, like the wall of some huge dome, closing in about them. High above was a torn and jagged

aperture through which they saw a deep black sky, the moon
and some brilliant stars. The moonlight was silent and cold,
it lifted the dark and cut a liquid path across the bay. Within
that streak they saw the boil of spume about the bodies of
trapped ships.

As they spoke their voices sounded strangely in the dark,
still vault of the night. The wall of motionless cloud seemed
to hold them captive at the base of a great white cup. It hung
before them over the sea, the mad gyration of the elements
locked away behind it. Only when they listened could they
hear again, faint and far away, the low moaning of the storm.
It was another world. They became conscious now of other
sounds: the odd, sudden movements of dropping, rustling,
scuttering noises, and sometimes the crack of twigs. But above
all it was water they heard, rushing and rapid.

Arthur shone his torch onto the road, and they saw the fast
reflective surface of a shallow flowing river. The narrow open
drains each side of the road that carried the water of mountain
springs and streams were engorged and blocked with debris
and overflowed the road. Under the light the steep descent
looked like a polished slide.

'It's not deep of course, but fast-moving and slippery. See
the children hold onto one another,' Arthur ordered. 'And
hurry. We have already wasted five minutes. Hurry.'

Slowly then, like an ungainly creature getting to its feet,
they grouped, drew breath, and set off from the orphanage gate.

13

Arthur led the way, his torch a long liquid snout before them. Eva illuminated the middle of the crocodile and Daniel backed up the rear. In the darkness their torches wheeled and cut like searchlights on the night. Arthur's feet were still bare in a pair of green plastic Japanese slippers; the water eddied and gushed about his heels, slipped over his feet and swam on. The toes of the slippers squelched and squeaked. He stumbled over a stone and almost lost his balance, the torch dipped and swayed precariously.

'Oh stop. Stop,' Eva shouted, for already a child was down and cried loudly. She picked her way across to Arthur. 'It's Ruriko, our blind one. She just can't get along like this, on her own. It will be much quicker, Mr Wilcox, if you carry her.' She emptied a wet quivering bundle of child into Arthur's arms. Her light turned and she was gone.

For a moment he dare not move, he had never held a small child before. It was not just her tininess that appalled him, but the independence of life within such a minute frame. He did not know if he could move. He felt the frailty of her weight in his arms and the throb of her body against him. The torch lit her face, her skin was the flesh of flowers. In the beam the pupils of her eyes did not contract, but stared at him, dilated and unseeing. Hesitantly he took a step and then another. He felt her arms fold round his neck and a small hand gently touch the contours of his face, climbing by the fingers over peaks and valleys. She pulled at the hair of his moustache.

'Is this your decoration? They told me about it.' The voice was small and sounded right in his ear. He jumped at hearing her speak. She slipped her fingers between his lips, feeling the crevice of his teeth. They touched his eyes, then delicately examined his nostrils. Something deep in him turned and uncoiled. His life was narrow as a cell, and the human touch was not included. The fingers returned to his moustache.

'What a lot of hair! How can you eat your food through it? On my birthday, last week, they tied a white bow in my hair. Do you tie bows on this?'

Arthur gave a gruff negative grunt. And something tightened in his throat, for she could not know what colour white was, and just repeated what she was told. A bow was a bow, was a shape in her hand, but white could mean nothing to her.

'If you don't hold me tighter I shall drop,' Ruriko informed him. Arthur nodded mutely and strengthened his grasp. The child gave a small sigh, tucked her head under his chin, and gave herself up to the ride. Arthur walked carefully forward, and rubbed his cheek gently on the silken head of the child. A strange soft tendril of emotion formed in his body, warm as the touch of velvet.

Before them was a surrealist landscape, black and twisted, gleaming under their torches. The dense trunks of trees flared up before them; torn branches and boulders strewed the road. The world was a slippery battered mess and lay like an exhausted body around them. The road swam underfoot.

Behind him Arthur heard the slap of the children's feet. Once he looked back in the dark, and saw the whole line of them in the torches' light stretched out behind him in a soggy array of pyjamas and dressing gowns, like a hurrying crocodile of midgets. They slowed behind his momentary pause and looked up in anxious question. He saw then his stature in their eyes, the immense conviction of belief in him. Ruriko moved her nose against his neck. All at once he felt like a clumsy Pied Piper in an Oriental Hamelin.

'Is everything all right there, Mr Wilcox?' Eva Kraig called anxiously.

'Tally ho!' Arthur waved his torch in the air, and lumbered on again.

They passed Mrs Okuno's house, shuttered and locked, a pile of dark shapes; she had gone to her daughter in Tokyo the night before. After the house one side of the road plunged steeply into a sharp ravine gaping black in the torchlight; a stream swilled somewhere down below, hardly audible above their own gushing road. On the other side the bank rose steeply. The wet trunks of trees, wrinkled and grey with mildew, were like the great stretching necks of reptiles now, unrecognisable. The air was thick with the smell of soaked undergrowth and leaves. The splash of small feet hurried diligently behind Arthur, who looked at his watch and quickened his pace as much as he dared on the slippery road.

'Hurry. We must hurry,' he shouted over his shoulder.

A crow rose up from the undergrowth with a loud flapping caw, and flew low over their heads like a great black moth. The movement of its wings stirred the motionless air.

Arthur heard the woman Kyo give a little scream. She was there not far behind, clothed again in her green cocktail dress, slipping and sliding with the rest. At the thought of her strength flowered in his blood. He relived again the few moments when he had pressed her to the wall, as the ceiling collapsed in the recreation room. Just the remembrance multiplied his will. He pulled himself up and drew fresh breath.

At that moment the torch picked up the barricade of his car across the road. Until he saw it before him, he had not given the car a thought since he left it near the orphanage gate. It had slithered down the flooded road, and now wedged against the bank, one wheel down the drain, a pile of wet debris stacked up against it. The fallen limb of a tree had dented the top and lay balanced upon the bonnet still. Arthur groaned at the sight, but could not stop.

The road was narrow, the recumbent car left only a single file track around it. Arthur led the way, holding tightly onto Ruriko. He felt a sudden tugging at his trouser leg, and looked down upon Hiroshi.

'Where's the carburettor?' Small eyes looked up at him.

'Get away,' responded Arthur roughly, shaking free his captive leg. But within him suddenly a finger of confusion bloomed into a strange regret. He looked down at the child and his plaster. 'I might show you. Maybe. After this typhoon. Can't promise.'

Hiroshi nodded sagely to this gentleman's agreement. And slapped his foot down with a splash that drenched Arthur's fingers round the torch.

Arthur turned back and trudged masterfully on. Soon he felt again a clutching at his trouser and a slight dragging weight as Hiroshi silently positioned himself and walked on beside him into the night. Above them the black hole in the moonlit clouds moved along its destined path.

14

Tottering ahead of Sister Elaine, Kyo stopped, tipped several small stones from her orphanage slipper and hurried on. She carried her spiky red shoes in her hand.

'Quickly. Quickly.' Arthur Wilcox's voice sounded back down the line. The children half ran, half walked, heads lowered, concentrating on their feet.

'Carefully. Hurry Nobuo. Itsuko, hold Masako's hand,' Eva called and encouraged.

The torchlight cut about tensely, illuminating the scurrying faces and figures, revealing Akiko's back, the crocheted border on Yoshiko's sleeve and the patched velvet ears of a rabbit Kimiko clutched. Its blue face and button eyes bobbed above the child's shoulder.

Sister Elaine half stumbled over a protruding log. The hem of her habit was heavy and wet, and wrapped about her knees. Her brogues squelched water. It was all madness. Madness. She could see, moment by moment, the black disc of sky above drifting slowly to their right. They would never make it. The scampering army of tiny legs, splashing along the streaming road, pulsated in her head. They should have stayed where they were. There was some chance, some protection there, but here, on this flooded road, there would be no hope. They would all be destroyed.

Set against the bank on the right the torches illuminated a *jizo-bosatsu*, a tiny wayside shrine, with its bald-headed deity to children. The cotton bibs of red and white, tied to the statue by bereaved mothers, were blown askew around his stone neck; the petals of offering flowers were battered far and wide. The children splashed by.

Before Sister Elaine ran the boy Kenichi. Every so often he looked up at the sky, fear in his eyes. As they ran, the slippery shapes of the night jerked up and down about Sister Elaine. The breath pounded in her chest; her body was a hollow cage knotting with her nerves. Liquid shadows streamed past and through them her flight cut a path, sinking and falling within a dark tunnel. It seemed the blackness of all the years behind turned tail and chased her now, washing down through the empty core of the storm. The road was steep and veered round each bend as if the ground was pulled suddenly from beneath. She was without hope. She was alone in a narrow passage.

Help us. Help me. God. But the words were limp in her mouth as never before. And she knew she was alone. Alone. She had reached an end.

As she ran now, her mind threw up weird fragments of memory, a rag-bag of unrelated snippets. She remembered the moss-covered wall of her childhood home, a farm in County Kerry. In a tumbledown house the other side of the wall lived the madwoman, Izzy O'Hara. Chickens and dogs roamed her one room, a pig sat in an armchair. She remembered the pig with its bald pink eyes, its naked piggy stare, that noticed yet ignored her. She remembered a knitted grey dishcloth she made for the poor in a convent near Dublin. She remembered the bared wet gums of the boy Kenichi, closed like a dog upon her wrist when he bit her the day before.

Unexpectedly then, she remembered the stained glass of the chapel in Osaka, where the wounds on Christ's figure on the cross flowered like a bunch of crimson grapes. Light streamed down upon her, sanctifying her hands with a gentle, rosy glow. The pictures slotted in and out of her mind, like the unreeling of a spool of film. They streamed behind her and mixed with the shadows, dissolving into the night.

She ran faster and faster, until it seemed she might take flight. And pass up and out of the ring of clouds like thread through the eye of a needle. Her heart bumped up and down, the memories jerked about in her head, sometimes leaving her like shooting stars to project on the sky in strange cloudy landscapes. There she saw again the yellow thickets of gorse and the snowy nets of hawthorn trees beyond the old farm wall. And growing clearer, firming slowly, emerged from them the face of the Reverend Mother years before. An old face, finely cracked like the glaze on ancient porcelain, and the white net of the hawthorn became the stiff white wings of her bonnet. We shall have to see. We shall have to see, she said in the voice of the Novice Mistress of long ago. When she spoke again it was the voice of the Bishop. What do you desire? In the face the old eyelids were wrinkled and lashless.

'Grace and mercy.' She cried the words aloud into the night. But they drowned beneath the splashing feet.

Run. Run. Run. The rhythm thumped in her head.

Run. Run. Run. She was unravelling like a ball of wool, her mind uncoiling loop by loop. She felt its slow disintegration, and a light-headed delirium seeping in. She had lost her mind, she had lost her faith. God had grown tired of her support. Or she had never supported Him enough. It no longer mattered. She was beyond hope and all redemption. The day before she had listed her sins in neat inked letters on a piece of blank white paper. She had rounded and carefully firmed each one, but in their little hieroglyphical list they looked alien and unimportant. The paper was still in the pocket of her habit. She crumpled it in her hand and it blew from her easily into the night, washed along the road, before being trodden under pounding feet.

Now everything in her was mixing and glittering and swirling together, like the tinsel bits of a kaleidoscope. As soon as a pattern formed in her mind it blew up and changed again.

She wished she was a bird.

Suddenly. Desperately.

Run. Run. Run. Faster. She was sure she could fly.

The small black circle of sky hovered high above. The crow returned again, flapped over their heads, then wheeled up and was lost. Why could she not fly? She thrust out her arms, propelling them up and down.

Run. Run. A strange exhilaration filled her. She began to laugh aloud, unburdening herself to the madness. The child, Kenichi, looked at her in fear, and the noise began behind her then.

A rushing, accompanied by the cracking of twigs, louder than the movement of water. A rumble, a slither. She heard the screams of the children. Suddenly the whole crocodile of bodies was parting and breaking around her, running confusedly in all directions. The torches slashed and parried in mid-air, their gleaming blades of light impotent before the collapsing bank of earth. Orders issued and voices mixed, discordantly.

The screams became louder. Before her a black mass of earth slid down upon the road, almost engulfing several of the children. Yoshiko shouted and snatched up Kimiko and with the other arm pulled Jun back from where he clung to a tree stump, already over the side of the road. The edge of the ravine veered suddenly up at Sister Elaine, like a deep wound in the dark beside her. The children slithered and fell, one clutched at the skirt of her habit. She was pushed suddenly off balance by

Eiko who lunged forward from behind to grab Tami and Toshio as they rolled into a heap to the very edge of the precipice. Then there was a loud confusion of fresh cries.

Sister Elaine looked behind and saw in the torchlight a great wave of mud and debris bearing down upon her. She screamed and stumbled against Kenichi, clutching him to her. The landslide descended upon them, sweeping them up in its cold wet mess.

She was sliding, rolling, turning. A clammy mush smothered her, mud and grit filled her mouth. Blunt objects jabbed her body, there were other small arms and legs mixed up with her own. She seemed to turn head over heels in a pulpy sea, falling. Falling. Something struck her on the chest and pain seared through her body. Then a wave of blackness claimed her.

15

She opened her eyes. The sky was a small black coin high above, and stared out of milky clouds. She saw now it was truly an eye, a dark, dilated pupil looking down, expressionless, upon her tattered bit of destiny.

She could not move. The heavy wetness of clothes plastered her body, the skirt of her habit was swaddled tightly round her legs. Each time she breathed a great pain thrust up in her chest. Wet mud caked her face and neck. It seemed she lay in a swampy grave. The moonlight was insipid, and when she tried to move she cried out in pain.

A jumble of voices replied, high and far away. She closed her eyes, still hearing the torrent and tumble of water nearby.

Turning her head she saw, only a few feet below where she lay, a swollen stream of water gushed.

From high above the light of torches swung down in long blades, searching. She saw a huddle of faces grouped behind them, and remembered a painting of angels' heads staring out of a break in clouds, pale emanating rays of light spilling out around them from Heaven to earth. Here all was darkness and mire. She wondered if she were in Hell, and for a moment was certain of it. Until she remembered the great wave of mud closing down upon her, and Kenichi pressed hard against her body. Slowly it came to her then that she lay somewhere at the bottom of the ravine, injured, for her body was filled with suffering, and seemed pinned beneath a weight. She called out again, and the sudden rush of breath knifed within her chest.

Voices replied once more, and the probing fingers of the torches swung frantically about, settling on her suddenly in a blaze of startling light. She drew a sharp breath and half closed her eyes, for in the light now she saw the black swell of a heavy branch across her feet, pinning her to the ground. Painfully lifting an arm, she tried to push it away, but her strength seemed gone, the branch did not move. Her hand slipped on its rough wet skin.

'Sister Elaine.' Eva's voice came from far away, a sound from another world, her mind felt numb to it. 'Daniel is coming down. Is Kenichi with you? Is he there?' The words were thrown to her, spaced and even and she struggled to retain them, to connect to the world above, using each word as a ladder. She looked up at the menacing eye of black sky in its sea of milky cloud, and remembered the desperate measure of each moment. Panic and life flowed into her. She tried to fight the pain and struggle free of the grip of the fallen branch. How long had she lain there? How long was there left? Listening then she heard again, faintly, the restless moan of the storm, waiting in ghostly wings to re-enter a battered stage. Above the sinister aperture moved on, imperceptibly, imperturbably.

'Kenichi. Is he with you, Sister Elaine?' Eva called again. But Sister Elaine was without the strength to answer. Each time she breathed under the weight of the branch pain seared her chest. It was punishment, just the beginning of something she had known must come, eventually. Just the beginning, of that she was sure. In the silver light of the moon the world had become a devious landscape, and she hoped she had not landed in purgatory. It was probably all that was left to her now.

She heard the noise, but took no notice until it came again, a scrabbling, moving sound. She could not turn to see, and lying there became afraid, aware of her vulnerability. She pictured some small animal pulling its way towards her, a rat, a weasel or a cat, and shivered, helpless. A twig cracked, a shower of small stones fell into the water. Something large was moving behind her, she felt its presence, nearer and nearer. Suddenly Kenichi spoke.

'Will they come in time?' He sat down beside her.

Above, the voices were active in discussion, the torchlight swung and jerked about, sometimes opening up upon them, sometimes leaving them in darkness. In a sudden frame of light she saw the child huddled beside her, clothed in a skin of mud. Tributaries of tears ran through the dirt of his face. She remembered again the globule of glistening spit on her red and bitten wrist, but felt no antagonism now.

'Do you think we shall die when the wind comes again?' he asked in a flat, even voice. Some strange fate had cast them

together, for what reason she did not know. His small life was
no less barren than her own, she understood that now. She felt
for the first time, in this dead black world, the uselessness of
summoning God. There was only herself and the child, rejected
and alone. Her fears, she realised suddenly, were no longer for
herself, but must include Kenichi, who squatted beside her.
With difficulty she reached out a hand and placed it on the
child's knee.

'They are coming down. They will rescue us. Until then we
must wait together.' She patted his thigh, and the child nodded
silently.

'Are you badly hurt? Can't you move?' he asked, looking at
the heavy log across her. Scrambling up suddenly, he started
pulling at the branch, but it barely moved and his agitation of it
made her groan. He knelt beside her again in concern.

'Are you all right? I can get it off you. I know a way.'

He twisted himself into an awkward contortion until his
neck and shoulders were beneath the low space under the log.
The torches spilt down suddenly upon them, like a spotlight,
cutting off the night, encircling them. The child began to push,
his muddy face contorted by the effort. His body was tense and
rigid, absorbed in pushing, his feet dug into the mud. Slowly he
began to rise. The light stayed on him, they were watching from
above. Beneath the mud his face grew purple and his eyes bulged
with the strain. At last he was up enough to kneel, the branch
lifted free of Sister Elaine and lay across the boy's shoulders. He
manoeuvred back, swivelling on his knees until he was clear of
Sister Elaine, then shrugged it off. It resounded on a rock and
rolled with a loud splash into the stream.

'Is that better? Can you move now?' he asked anxiously,

coming back to kneel beside her.

It was easier, the pressure was gone, the pain was a fraction less. 'I think I have broken some ribs,' she said. She could still hardly move, and took shallow breaths, unable to inhale deeply. The child's face was close to her. Its dark shape struggled to open and communicate.

'Does it hurt very much?'

She only nodded, not wishing to alarm him. And wondered again why they had both been thrown here against their will to share the same abandonment. It seemed strange that they, who only moments before, in another dimension on a flooded road, faced each other in contempt, should now, on this marshy shelf, draw together as allies.

'Shall I help you sit up?' His dark eyes, so close to her own, both asked and answered his unanswerable questions. The tight glaze of defence was gone, she saw now a small and delicate face, watching her. A face in which everything that must happen had already happened, too soon. The weight of experience already shaped his response to life for better or for worse.

She tried to murmur comfort, but heard herself utter only a few limp words. The distances in life had always overcome her. She knew no way to unlock other people, for she herself had never opened. Lying there she felt ashamed, that it was the child who came to her. Tears roughened her eyes.

'I don't think I can move. We must just wait. And pray.' The last word was only habit. It seemed suddenly of more use to put out a hand, and cover the child's small fingers.

'They're coming down now. It won't be long. Look.'

They saw Daniel swing over the edge of the ravine, a torch hung round his neck, and begin to feel his way down, hanging precariously, high above them. The light and faces at the edge of the ravine turned away and vanished, leaving only darkness and the moving spot of Daniel's torch.

'Go on. Go. Hurry.' They heard him shout upwards to a lingering voice.

The small fingers under Sister Elaine's hand turned up a warm palm and responded with a grip. She shook it gently.

'We'll be all right, I'm sure.' The words sounded more convincing now.

They waited together in the dark, straining their eyes on the descending light, bobbing and swaying. Above them all the black orifice moved on.

16

Daniel lost his grip, and fell the last few feet, landing awkwardly on the mess of debris within which lay Sister Elaine, half buried still, Kenichi beside her. He flashed his light upon them and saw their relief.

'Are you badly hurt?' He knelt beside Sister Elaine digging about her with his bare hands.

'There, can you move your legs?' He sat back on his haunches, the large face of the torch breaking open the grim black landscape about them.

Now they could see the mound of branches, rock and mud that had swallowed them. The arms of shrubs stuck out at twisted angles, like battered limbs. The body of a dead rat lay near Sister Elaine, plastered with mud, small teeth bared in its open mouth, its belly split and bloody. She shivered and looked away.

Hesitantly she moved her legs and found them free and whole.

'It's my ribs, I think something is broken,' she apologised.

'Oh Jesus. We've only got five minutes left.' Daniel shone the torch on the angry stream coursing beside them.

'What'll happen to us? How will we climb up?' Kenichi anxiously asked.

'We can't climb back. What we're going to do is follow the stream. We're already at the bottom here. Round that bend Eva says the stream meets with the road again near the Coopers' house. They'll meet us there, or Mr Wilcox will wait for us. I hope they make it in time, they have the whole shoulder of the hill to cover. If we can manage the water it should not take us long. Come on, we must hurry.' Daniel put his arm beneath Sister Elaine's shoulders.

'Can you stand? Good. This is going to be painful, but you'll have to try. It's our only chance.' Sister Elaine stood unsurely, each time she breathed or moved the pain was excruciating. Daniel flashed the torch on the rushing water, then stepped down into it and steadied himself against the strong current, clinging to the side of the bank as the water pushed hard against him.

'Come on.' He took Kenichi's hand first and helped him down.

'Keep near the bank, hold on. Sister Elaine, take my hand.' He held his arm out to her.

She hobbled painfully forward.

'I can't,' she said, looking down into the swilling water.

'There's no other way. You must try. Come on.'

The pain shot about in her body, like hot knives ripping her flesh. She took his hand and with effort pushed herself forward and down into the cold thrusting water. The jolt of the step made her faint with pain and she collapsed to her knees in the stream. The water threw itself upon her, beating her chest, she doubled up and groaned in agony.

'Kenichi, you'll have to take this and guide us.' Daniel handed the torch to the boy, then turned to Sister Elaine, helping her to her feet again. 'I'll carry you.'

She nodded and braced herself, but cried out in pain as he lifted her and held her cradled against him. He turned into the stream, and shouted suddenly.

'Hey. Where are you going? Come back!'

Kenichi was clambering with the torch out of the stream, running to where they had come from. He picked up some object and came panting back to them again.

'It's Kimiko's rabbit. Look.' He held the soggy, battered blue body of the rabbit up to their inspection.

'Never mind, come on. Quick,' shouted Daniel. 'Keep to the bank, off you go, Kenichi.'

They started, the child feeling the way carefully, shouting out the location of rocks or fallen debris, turning and flashing the torch on the water for them. Once he stumbled and went under, came up gasping and struggled on again. In places, to arrest a steep incline, the bed of the stream was shaped in shallow steps, and these Daniel negotiated slowly, sometimes standing Sister Elaine in the water, and lifting her up again after stepping down the few inches. The water swirled angrily about them, writhing and sucking as if to devour them, pushing into the backs of their knees. The child hung onto shrubs from the bank, the rabbit tucked under his torch carrying arm. He shouted information and encouragement over his shoulder. They passed under a railway bridge and their voices echoed hollowly in the damp

stony vault, water dripped on their heads. As they emerged they
saw in the torchlight the main road ahead, and the crocodile of
children above them on a bridge. They waved and shouted. Eva
came to the rail and waited until they were beneath it.

'There is a ladder in the wall the other side. You'll have to
cross the stream. We'll wait for you there.' Her face was a small
floodlit sphere high above them.

'Okay,' Daniel shouted, Kenichi flashed the torch across the
stream picking out the wet metal rungs of the ladder in the side
of the bank. On the iron footbridge above, the children's feet
rattled as they hurried across.

'Keep near, hold onto me, Kenichi. The current will be
stronger out there,' Daniel shouted.

At this lower point the stream spread out wider. The water
was shallower, but the current ran hard, like sinewy ligaments
straining in the water. Once a clump of weeds tangled about
Daniel's foot and he stumbled forwards. The weight of the
clinging Kenichi steadied him and he straightened again.

Sister Elaine bit her lips until blood ran in her mouth with
a warm metallic taste. The pain twisted within her, at each step
Daniel took she winced and suppressed a cry, his arm about her
was like a rack. Sometimes she opened her eyes and followed the
black aperture of sky, until it began to break and dissolve. Then
the few stars flickered and disappeared. The sky was moving and
troubled again, the moon had vanished. Darkness piled down
upon them, muttering. She felt the first wind upon her face.

'It has started again,' she sobbed in terror. Daniel stopped in
mid-stream, looking up at the sky. They heard far off, growing
nearer a sound like an army approaching, throbbing and
drumming, a vicious beat.

'Come on.' The shout was from across the stream, lights clustered at the top of the ladder.

'Go on. Go ahead. Run.' Daniel shouted and the lights bobbed and dipped and dispersed in reply, leaving blackness again.

They thrust on across the stream, their bodies filled now by the pulse of the returning storm. Fingers of wind grew stronger, and lifted strands of hair, stroking their faces. Daniel was half running now, the weight of the woman a painful strain on his arms. Sister Elaine clung to him, whimpering. They reached the ladder and above it a tiny eye of light hovered like a glow worm.

'I'm here.' Arthur Wilcox's voice came to them. 'The others have gone ahead, they must already be safe.' His pencil torch weaved about above them.

'Thank God. Kenichi, quick, up you go,' Daniel ordered the child. It was raining now, great flat spots. The wind moaned like an animal.

Arthur Wilcox reached down and pulled Kenichi up the last few ladder rungs. 'Hurry. Hurry.'

'Come on. Up you go, Sister Elaine. I'm here behind you. I'll push you.' Daniel lifted her onto the ladder.

The drag on her arms was unbearable, as if her body was being sucked out through them, twisted slowly by the sinews. The pain in her chest jabbed and sawed, her head throbbed and nausea filled her. With the pull of each effort upwards her head reeled, but she felt the support of Daniel's shoulder beneath her hips as he pushed her upwards. Slowly, the top of the ladder and the road came nearer. Arthur Wilcox's face leaned over, his arms reached down and gripped her, pulling her up. She cried out with the pain and fainted.

The wind played with the rain, whipping it angrily, then letting it fall quickly and flatly. The gale weaved about restlessly.

Daniel pulled himself over the edge of the ladder, and as if it waited for that moment the wind released itself suddenly, hard as a brick slammed down upon them. Daniel gasped and swayed back on the ladder. The rain emptied down in a solid sheet, thrashing against them, each drop sharp as flint.

'Run, run,' Arthur shouted. He picked up the unconscious woman, heaved her over his shoulder in a fireman's clasp and galloped off ahead of them.

Rain and wind pushed against them now like an unrelenting board, nearly throwing them off balance.

'Jesus,' muttered Daniel over and over again. He put his hand on Kenichi's shoulder as they ran to anchor him, afraid he might be blown away. They kept their bodies bent and low, thrusting their heads out before them. Ahead Arthur staggered on with his bundle. Sister Elaine's arm swung free and limp like a pendulum.

A soggy remnant of newspaper slapped suddenly onto Daniel's face, filling his mouth and nostrils with the wet stale taste of fish. He spat and tore it free, and lifting his head too high, was nearly blown over. A clump of dry shrub blew by and vanished. Somewhere near was the shatter of glass.

'Hurry. Hurry,' Arthur shouted back. They saw the house ahead of them now, the great automatic copper doors drawn back, open and waiting.

Behind the windows of the house was the comfort of candle glow. They struggled towards it and coming through the gate saw a mass of familiar faces clustered about the door. A great cry went up as they appeared; arms and tears received them. The copper gate swung shut with a clang. Kenichi began to cry.

Part Three

THE
LAST QUADRANT

1

Geraldine Cooper gave little screams of concern and hopped about in a bird-like way from one group of destitutes to another. She tried not to see the mud on her wall-to-wall beige carpet. She divided the twenty-five children between four marble bathrooms and ordered the wetter articles of clothing deposited in the bathtubs. Sister Elaine she relegated to the larger guestroom. She decided against the magnanimity of her own bed, after reviewing the state of the nun's habit. She bustled them all upstairs and, throwing open her cupboards, produced towels enough for an army.

After mopping and inspection most children had lost an outer layer; the younger were divested of their under ones too, and stood shivering, knees knocking in the sudden cold. Geraldine stopped only to think, a finger to her cheek. She delved into closets and chests until she amassed an enormous pile of cardigans and sweaters.

'I never throw out, there's always a need,' she said, her arms full, her chin holding steady a top-heavy pile of clothes, which she dumped on the parquet-floored landing. She hurried back for more. Soon the mezzanine and upper landings were crowded with children around the soft heap of Geraldine's garments.

'Come along. Take your pick.' Geraldine spread her arms above the litter of her wardrobe. The children came forward hesitantly, fishing out colours and textures that appealed.

'It smells nice.' Emiko buried her nose in the sleeve of a cashmere sweater. Geraldine bent to confirm.

'*L 'Air du Temps*. My favourite.'

'This one smells too. I'm not a girl,' Nobuo said in disgust. Geraldine bent again.

'*Je Reviens*. Very expensive,' she pronounced.

'I said I'm not a girl.' Nobuo threw down the sweater.

'Nothing else, poppet. You'll have to grin and bear it, after all this is an emergency.' Geraldine moved to where Eiko Kubo pulled an angora tube over Ruriko's head.

Soon the children were clothed and ran about in strange array, first-aid plaster patches adorning their naked legs. Yoshiko Mori and Eiko Kubo began to giggle. Nobuo's head rose contemptuously above fluffy pink mohair and pearl buttons. One or two smaller children appeared to be handless within the droop of long sleeves.

Standing back, Geraldine surveyed the familiar bits of her wardrobe that seemed suddenly to have sprouted heads and short spindly legs and danced about as if brought to life in a nightmare. Occasionally a favourite piece skipped by, whose sacrifice she somewhat regretted. But she reminded herself of the emergency.

'Come along, come along.' She led them downstairs with the help of Yoshiko and Eiko. Eva and Akiko were attending to Sister Elaine.

But Toshio, numb and petrified with fear, stood helpless in

a green cardigan. Kimiko clung to him, whimpering, equally shaken. Tami ran back ahead of Yoshiko, and picked up the silent Toshio, too terrified to cry. She hauled him across the floor.

'Give him to me,' said Yoshiko. 'You can't manage him, Tami, down those stairs. Here, take Ruriko's hand.'

Fear was easing in the other children; some were buoyant with relief. They trooped behind Geraldine, feet vibrating on the stairs. They followed her into the lounge and quietened suddenly, subdued by that massive room with its wall of plate glass window, looking onto a pillared patio and colonnade. Inside, a huge three-cornered fireplace divided the open room from the dining area at a lower level.

Arthur and Daniel sipped drinks Nate Cooper had quickly given them. There were another three guests in the room, a woman and two men. In the middle of the lounge one of the men played upon a grand piano; a shower of notes cascaded from it. He stopped as Geraldine and the children came in.

'Do go on, Dennis, I'm sure the children would enjoy the music,' said Geraldine. 'Maybe you know some nursery rhymes?' The man looked apprehensive. Beside him, leaning against the piano stood Kyo, revived by a glass of whisky. She hummed a little tune during the pause in the music, the green lace dress and her hair were bedraggled, mud covered her legs and feet.

'Who's that?' hissed Geraldine as Eva appeared suddenly in the lounge.

'That's Kyo. She was visiting us, she used to work in the orphanage.' Eva hoped she had squashed all questions.

'Not quite your usual type, is she, dear?' Geraldine decided, and eyed Kyo disapprovingly.

'A little drink, Dr Kraig? You all need a drop after such an ordeal. Or would you prefer something hot?' Nate Cooper fussed over Eva, a hand familiarly on her arm.

'I've already told the maid to get hot drinks and some food for the children. The poor loves must be exhausted, not to mention terrified,' Geraldine told Eva.

'Let me introduce you to our other guests, victims of the storm like you, Dr Kraig,' Nate Cooper announced. 'Now, this is Hartley Rover of Chase Manhattan. This is Annette Rouleau of the Rouleau Gallery, and at the piano is Dennis Denzel of the British Consulate.' Hartley and Annette shook Eva's hand, Dennis Denzel bowed from the piano which now released Beethoven's *Moonlight Sonata*. Some of the children already gathered about him, and he looked at Eva over their heads.

'We're all waifs of the storm, Dr Kraig. Thank God for the Coopers and their magnanimous shelter.' Dennis Denzel gave Geraldine a solemn bow.

'Oh a pleasure,' trilled Geraldine. 'They knew the typhoon was about, but hadn't heard it was coming to Kobe, Eva.'

'Well, few of them come this way. The usual course is Wakayama, across the bay,' Annette put in. 'We simply never thought. We had all been to a new fish restaurant Dennis had found somewhere in the wilds, I couldn't even tell you where, Dennis always finds these places. They were shutting up when we arrived, because of the typhoon. They served us as a special favour. We thought we'd get back in time. It's all Dennis's fault,' she said petulantly. 'Hart and I were set for a cosy dinner together in my flat, before Dennis dragged us out.' Annette put a possessive arm through Hartley's. She spoke with an American accent in spite of her name. Her face was a slit in long blond hair and she puffed at a black Russian cigarette.

'Well, we sure are proud to be here to welcome you at the end of your epic adventure,' smiled Hartley Rover. His shirt was partly unbuttoned, a gold medallion and a chain nestled on his hairy chest. At his side Kimiko stopped staring at him and began to whimper again.

'Oh no. There, there.' Hartley bent and picked her up. 'Hey, aren't you cute? Isn't she, Annette?' Annette Rouleau backed away, placing a nervous hand on the assortment of silverware settled on the breast of her long silk caftan.

'Now, Eva, what will you have to drink? A brandy, or a bourbon,' Nate Cooper insisted.

'Well I really don't drink, but I would like a coffee. I came down because of Sister Elaine. She has broken some ribs, do you have anything I can bind her up with, an old sheet I can tear up would be best.'

'A sheet? No problem, Eva dear,' Geraldine cried. In the numerous lights of the ceiling, the pearls feasted at her neck.

'Rip up the sheets? Now, that should loose a few inhibitions.' Dennis Denzel left the piano and came to stand beside them. His eyes were reduced behind thick glasses, his voice was a thin nasal prong. He wore a purple velvet jacket, and a flamboyant flowered cravat.

Junko had begun to shift impatiently on her toes. She turned a couple of pirouettes about Dennis Denzel's legs, then looked up at him obliquely.

'Play the song about the crow,' she ordered.

'Crow ... well ... I don't know any Japanese children's songs, young lady. How does it go?' He bent down to her as his glasses slipped forward on his nose.

'*Karasu naze naku no. Karasu wa yama ni ...*' Junko's small voice rose to a high crescendo, and the children looked at Dennis hopefully.

'*Karasu ... yes ...* well, I don't actually know it. But we might be able to improvise something.' Dennis walked back to the piano holding Junko's hand and some of the smaller children followed. Dennis sat down and tried the keys. Junko nodded at the appropriate notes, and a few small voices began to sing.

'A sing song. Say, how about that?' Hartley questioned Kimiko, still in his arms. He glanced at Tami and Toshio standing to one side. 'What's your name?' he said, looking at Toshio's terrified face and the shiver that shook the child.

'Toshio,' Tami answered for him.

'You know that song?' Hartley asked him, the child nodded dumbly after a moment.

'You'll have to teach me. How does it go? *Karasu ...*' Hartley stopped to take Toshio's hand and still carrying Kimiko, turned to Dennis at the piano. He looked at Annette over his shoulder. 'Come on now Annette, grab a child, can't you? These kids have been through a lot.'

But Annette Rouleau just looked at him coldly. Hartley Rover shrugged, and walked off with the children to the piano. Eiko Kubo and Yoshiko Mori followed with the others. At the invasion Kyo retreated from the piano to a corner of the room, and drank down the rest of her whisky. Then she looked towards the open bottle Nate had left on the bamboo bar.

'Just let me check the ptoceedings in the kitchen, then I'll get you the sheet, Eva dear,' said Geraldine. She turned to the group at the piano. 'I've all kinds of treats I know I can find. Won't it be fun now, a midnight feast in the middle of a typhoon,'

Geraldine told the children as she frisked about amongst them, her skirts lifted and her décolletage gaping. She threw herself into the principal role, her voice cracking sometimes in excitement.

Some children began to venture into the deeper regions of the room and gathered wonderingly about the three-faced fireplace with its token fire of smouldering logs.

'It's not winter yet; it's not even cold,' Mariko and Yumiko questioned each other.

'It's one of the advantages of air-conditioning, dear. We can have a fire in the middle of summer. I thought it would be so cosy in the typhoon, but the wind blows down the chimney. I couldn't manage more than those two logs.'

Nate Cooper pulled forward a chair for Eva, as Geraldine hurried into the kitchen issuing orders loudly inside to the maid.

'Beats me how all you folk managed not to hear of the typhoon. We'd been keeping track of it all day. I can tell you I'm nervous here on the sea front. Of course they warned me when I built. They would have evacuated us if the typhoon's course had not changed so abruptly. When we realised it was too late to leave. I'm saying my prayers, I can tell you. The lights went a while back, but we've got a great stock of candles as you can see, and the house will see us through; we thought of everything when we built it. Guess you could say this little place is a veritable fortress, yes indeed.' Nate Cooper took a quick sip from his drink.

Hiroshi ran up to the window and observed the machinations of the typhoon. In the bare walled garden facing the sea there was little by which to gauge the typhoon, compared to the wooded slope of the orphanage. Even the noise was turned down behind soundproofed walls. Hiroshi banged his plaster cast arm on the wall of glass.

'It'll be your plaster that breaks on that, kid,' Nate Cooper said, amused. 'Imported from Sweden, real thick plate glass. Stand up to anything.' Hiroshi looked at Nate apprehensively, and then ran back to the group at the piano.

'*Karasu ...*' Hartley sang in unison with Dennis Denzel as the children's voices rose about them. Eva smiled.

'I'm terribly sorry about the mud stains on your carpet,' she apologised to Nate.

'Oh, come now,' said Nate expansively. 'What are a few mud stains between friends?'

About the piano the children relaxed. Even Toshio moved his lips to a few words of song under Tami's dogged encouragement. On the perimeter of the dining area Jun and Takeo wheeled as nosediving aeroplanes and coughed up their lungs as they crashed from the step. Annette Rouleau huddled into a nearby chair looking pained, and puffed on her black cigarette. She hugged her glass for safety high upon her silverware.

'Children... children,' Eva called to quieten them and apologised to Nate again. 'It's been such a ghastly night, they're quite beside themselves.'

Geraldine came out of the kitchen. 'Everything's under control, now let's see about that sheet.'

'I could help in there, instead,' Eiko Kubo said as Eva stood up, and went through into the kitchen.

Eva followed Geraldine to the stairs. At the window of the lounge Daniel flashed a strong torch out into the night. She saw the beam light up the lawn, boggy with water, littered with uprooted shrubs and dwarf trees. A pile of ornate iron garden furniture was stacked to one side of the patio; it collapsed with a crash as Eva watched. The voices of the singing children filled the lounge, but outside the sea rose up in white brimmed peaks some way beyond the garden wall, thrashing and pounding. A branch of flowering bush was thrown with a thud against the window in a shower of petals and soil. It fell and was swept up again, leaving muddy marks on the glass.

Eva looked away and hurried after Geraldine.

2

'Geraldine,' Maud Bingham called for her daughter.

It was the most terrible night. Old Maud Bingham shivered in her bed; she had never seen such a storm. The wind was like some heinous creature ploughing, invisible, into the house, hysterical because it could find no chink of entry. A sudden flash of lightning illuminated the rain, so that she could see the whole mad woven pattern of it. Thank God, she thought, Nate had settled for a garden of stunted Japanese trees. She would not have liked to be up in the hills tonight, back in the old house, surrounded by pines and steep inclines. Nevertheless, here they had the sea. It foamed up in huge waves, crashing upon the sea-wall, flooding the road. And that was what she feared: flooding. For in that flash of lightning she had seen the waves rearing up, like great long-haired monsters from the deep. Several times the broken bodies of birds had slammed against the glass, and once a branch of the camellia bush, uprooted from the garden. Now as she watched some hard object was flung upon the window. The cracking thud of it beat in her head, and she cried out aloud.

'Geraldine.' The world moaned and screamed in answer.

It seemed her mind had also turned, for beyond the closed door the house was alive with unfamiliar noises. She heard a great pounding up and down the stairs of feet, and strange high voices that sounded like children, a senseless jumble of sound melting in her head with the monstrous storm. It was the evil night, that had awoken the spirits of the dead and sent them into the world of the living. Her throat dried in terror. 'Geraldine. Geraldine.'

The door opened. It was Geraldine and a man. 'Draw the curtains, Geraldine. Draw them, quick. For I cannot watch it any longer. Oh, how frightened I have been. Once I thought it over, everything stopped, it went quite calm. But it started again. Oh, so much worse, as if it would murder us all.'

'Poor Mother,' said Geraldine soothingly. 'In all the excitement I quite forgot her. We have a whole orphanage here tonight, Mother. Eva Kraig's orphanage, fled down from the hill and some dreadful things.'

'What? What did you say, Geraldine?'

'Never mind, never mind. Now, look Mother who I have brought to see you. Mr Wilcox, father's friend.'

'Wilcox? Wilcox? Never heard of him.' Maud Bingham expelled her false teeth into her hand. 'You forgot to help me take them out after dinner,' she complained. Her lips sank in upon her gums and lay gathered like slack leather.

'Mr Wilcox, Mother, used to play billiards with Father in the club.' Geraldine dropped the teeth in a glass of water. A speck of cabbage floated free.

'*Clair de lune*, madam. We always ended an evening with *Clair de lune*. I accompanied you on the flute. Surely you remember those wonderful evenings, all Kobe used to come.'

'Flute? *Clair de lune*? That was young Arthur. Always played off tune. Can't remember a Wilcox.'

The curtains were drawn now, the candle sent shadows skating over the walls and there was a warm glow. She began to relax, the dryness eased from her throat.

'I am he, madam. I am he, young Arthur.' He moved about on his toes at the memory of his youthfulness.

Maud scrutinised him suspiciously. 'Young Arthur had no moustache. Young Arthur was red-headed.'

'Alas, madam. Time moves on.' He stroked his grey hair.

'Now, Mother, Mr Wilcox is writing a little pamphlet for the centenary of the club. After that he is going to write a history of the foreign community in Kobe. Now, isn't that exciting? Mr Wilcox thinks you might be able to provide him with a lot of material, Mother. He is anxious to have a talk with you about old times.' Geraldine bent near her mother's ear, speaking loudly. Arthur observed the lustrous collar of pearls about her neck and the dark dividing wedge in the scoop of her low-cut dress.

'Well, I can't say it wouldn't be pleasant to have someone to talk to me for once. Old times, eh? Well, come here then young Arthur, or Wilcox, or whoever you are.' Maud patted the bed beside her and fussed at a ribbon under her chin. Her teeth watched, suspended, in an endless smile from the glass beside her bed.

3

The candle went out as they finished binding up Sister Elaine's broken rib.

'There are no matches here, I'll go down,' said Akiko.

'I'd better come too. The children must be running wild. Will you be all right now, Sister Elaine? Just lie quietly, try not to move,' Eva instructed. She and Akiko groped their way from the dark room.

The blackness settled about Sister Elaine, but it was not like the darkness of the wild night outside; this darkness was restful and supportive. She felt emptied, as if some solid thing had been squeezed from her. She could not explain; the world seemed remade. It felt like her cheek was touching the pillow for the first time. She sighed at the end of her tight swaddled body. Outside, somewhere distant, the wind battled on. She shut her eyes and slept.

Small bobbing flames and the closing of the door woke her. They walked in a line towards her, three of them. The flames of the candles cracked the black room and soft blurred shadows melted the walls. Their faces appeared skeletal, like ancient manikins above the lights.

'We brought you some candles,' said Kenichi. Behind him the small figure of Kimiko clutched a soggy blue rabbit. She held it up to Sister Elaine.

'Kenichi saved it. He's my friend now.'

Jiro carried a second candle. 'They all want to be his friend now. I have drawn a picture of you at the bottom of the ravine.'

They stood the candles on the bedside table and a shelf. The room smelled suddenly of melting wax, shadows moved fluidly to the rhythm of the flames. The wind swelled on outside, within it great fractured crashing sounds that were the boil of the sea and waves. Jiro went to the window and pulled open the curtains a slit. Light from the room behind him lit part of the view.

'The sea is all over the road, the waves are huge. It looks like part of the sea-wall has broken, everywhere is flooded,' he said excitedly, repeating possibilities he had heard the adults discussing.

'Come away. Don't watch, don't worry. We're all safe now. Nothing can happen,' said Sister Elaine.

'Does it still hurt?' Kenichi asked. She nodded.

'But not quite so much. They have bandaged me up very tightly,' she told him. He seemed a different child, aggression was gone from his face; the other children had made a hero of him.

'*We* all wanted to come up to see you. But they said only three of us could come. *We* were chosen,' Kenichi said gravely, stressing the *we* with pride. He was dressed in a shaggy heather sweater from which his legs obtruded nudely. Jiro wore a similar article in lemon yellow and Kimiko was lavishly attired in beaded black angora. Sister Elaine began to laugh and stopped at once in pain.

The children watched her with an equal interest. She was clothed in one of Maud Bingham's flannel nightdresses, her mud-plastered habit and veil removed to the nearest bath tub. A bright floral scarf of Geraldine's was tied about her head. She did not mind their staring.

'Do I look funny?' She smiled at them.

'Not funny. Different,' Jiro answered diplomatically. 'Shall I show you my drawing?'

They sat beside her on the bed as Sister Elaine rested the open sketchbook on her chest. They waited in silent expectation. The dark forms of purgatory were before her again on the page. There was the river, sinuous and dense with textured currents beneath the black eye of the sky. Diminished and helpless within the darkness lay a small white bundle with a veil, the stick-like form of a child and a toy rabbit. All the figures were small and lost in the bold thick lines of earth and sky. It reminded her of Munch.

'Yes,' she said quietly. 'Yes, we are all there.'

It stuck in her anew, how close they had been to disaster. She looked at the faces pressed about her. In the flickering candlelight the three sets of eyes were dark and polished as wet stones, anxious and friendly. She stared as if seeing them for the first time.

Why? Why was I saved? Why am I given the faces of these children, who have come to me like this, she thought. But the answer was there already in herself, like a pulse that glowed and beat in her breast. A feeling she thought she had lost. In the silent semicircle of eyes, something, it seemed, was being explained. She understood the answer although she could not yet comprehend the words. She closed her eyes on tears, then opened them on the sketch.

'May I keep it?' she asked. 'To remind me.'

The children nodded gravely, and Jiro tore out the page from the book.

4

The room flared with the candle on the bedside table in Maud Bingham's room. Her skin glowed like ancient parchment stretched over the bones of her face. The flickering light cast her cadaverously, but her eyes were stirred and bright.

'There was that time, young Arthur, do you not remember,

when the club was accused of lese-majesty, because it was found that a particular flower, introduced into the wooden carved post of the grand staircase, bore some resemblance to the Imperial Chrysanthemum Crest. Oh yes. I remember it well.

'Oh it is so good to talk to you again, young Arthur. How I wish dear Horace was with us just now. We could strike up once more with *Clair de lune*. La laa la laa ...' Maud Bingham lay back, eyes closed upon the pillow, conducting gently with a withered hand. She felt deep and warmed inside. It was almost as if she was back again within those jewelled days. How nice of young Arthur to visit her.

'By Jove, madam. Maud, yes. I may call you Maud again, may I not? For you did allow me that liberty once. Yes, good idea of Geraldine's, that I should come and talk to you. Makes all the memories come racing back.

'That chap who built the club, dashed short-sighted of him to throw in a royal chrysanthemum.' Arthur scribbled hurried notes on paper supplied by Geraldine.

'How I wish, young Arthur, you would expand to a history of the foreign community in Tokyo and Yokohama, where I grew up. For I have just remembered the balloon ascent in the field across from our old home. I was barely seventeen. We watched from our balconies. We had a great number of guests, we passed around tea and persimmon cake. Our foreign faces and habits were a great oddity to the people on the field. They kept looking at us through their opera glasses and telescopes. We had to put up our bamboo blinds. Oh, and you should have seen the balloon. I have never set eyes on anything so huge, and made all of purple silk. I remember it as if it were yesterday, but how I do run on. Now tell me, young Arthur, about your billiards. Did you let Horace beat you again?'

Arthur stretched his neck uncomfortably in the collar of his shirt. He was suddenly unsure of the shadowy room, and the animated skeleton in the bed.

'Now, where were we?' Maud Bingham closed her eyes on the pillow to rest for a moment from the sheer excitement of her memories. Her heart was throbbing, she felt years younger.

'Do you know, young Arthur, Kobe has honourable mention by at least two famous writers. Rudyard Kipling in *From Sea to Sea*, devoted a page of praise to the original Oriental Hotel. And Somerset Maugham in a story called *A Friend in Need*, writes about the Tarumi beacon and some members of the old foreign community.'

Her body was liquid inside, her limbs seemed no longer stiff. The blood raced in her veins with the memories and she closed her eyes to contain it all, for suddenly she felt a great fatigue. It was as if some whole sealed section of her mind had been blasted open. And the memories, like multicoloured confetti, swirled up in clouds, the light catching on their many facets, showering and dazzling and exhausting her. She settled her head more comfortably on the pillow and immediately fell asleep. Arthur Wilcox waited politely several minutes, and then tiptoed from the room.

5

The lounge moved and shimmered alive with the eyes of many candles. Nate Cooper and Daniel had the bigger boys organised in their distribution, directing them about the house.

In the lounge heat and light radiated out, a smell of hot wax smouldered; without electricity and air-conditioning the room was growing hot.

On the grand piano Dennis Denzel impressed his audience with the virtuosity of some Greig. Chords thundered and rattled like ammunition into the room, nearby candles shuddered, one on the piano top collapsed. There were squeals from the children, Eiko picked it up quickly and rubbed off warm wax with a fingernail. Eyes closed and body swaying, Dennis Denzel failed to notice. About him candles trembled on.

Yoshiko emerged through the swing door of the kitchen with a tray of Coca-Cola. The word went round immediately. The orphans hurried forward and Dennis Denzel was left alone with Greig.

'Don't riot,' laughed Yoshiko, the strain easing for a moment in her face.

'Now, here we are.' Geraldine came out of the kitchen followed by a maid. They placed platters of sandwiches and cake on the table. 'Now, here are paper plates and napkins. Don't wipe your hands on the furniture.' The children crowded about her at the table. Hiroshi pushed himself to the front, using his plaster arm as a lever through the crush.

'You're a rude boy. You should let the smaller ones go first,' Tami scolded. 'Let Toshio go first. Come along Toshio.' She pushed the child up to Geraldine, who gave him a plate. Tamiko began to pile it with sandwiches and cake.

'No more, Tami, he'll be sick. The others have also to eat,' Eva said, steering Ruriko forward to a chair.

'But the typhoon has made him hungry,' Tamiko insisted. 'Hasn't it, Toshio?' Toshio nodded obediently, his face was streaked and dirty with tears, his eyes were small and tired. In a corner Eva noticed Kimiko already curled up asleep.

'We must get some of you to sleep after this,' she decided.

'No. No,' Nobuo, Takeo and Jun spoke out together. 'We want to stay up all night.'

'All night?' Eva questioned in mock horror. 'After all this?'

'*All* night,' they insisted stoutly.

Kimiko had curled up with a cushion on the floor. Annette Rouleau moved a foot to avoid contact with her, shrinking back into a corner of the settee, nervously fingering the silver pendants hanging from her numerous chains. Hartley came up and sat beside her. He looked down at Kimiko. 'Poor kid, she's exhausted.'

'Get me another drink, Hart.'

'Now, Annette.'

'Oh come on Hart, give me a break.' Annette's face twitched in agitation. Hartley got up, shaking his head, and came back with a fresh gin and tonic.

'Christ, Hart, when is this going to end? Have we got to put up with these kids all night? Why don't they get them to bed?'

'I guess they will as soon as they can. Can't you understand what these kids have been through? They've got to eat, they've got to unwind before they'll settle to sleep, except for the smallest of them.' He nodded at the exhausted Kimiko. 'Pull yourself together, Annette. They could use an extra hand, why don't you do something to help? Look at Dennis, playing his heart out for them there.'

'I can't,' said Annette. 'I've got pains in my stomach, I feel quite ill, Hart. And you know I can't stand children. There is nothing I should be able to do.'

'Get a hold on yourself, that's all you need do. Think of the others instead of yourself, that'll clear up your pains,' Hartley said impatiently. He began to wonder what had drawn him to Annette in the first place. He looked at her hard, but Annette was staring in terror again at the wall of glass that impaled them upon the night, spreading the typhoon before them as if on a cinema screen.

'Christ, Hart, why can't she draw the curtains?' Annette's voice rose as a sod of earth was hurled against the window.

'She told you, they've gone for dry cleaning. We're all feeling like you, Annette, we're all nervous. You're not the only one, you've got to control it.' Hartley stood up, walking off to Dennis who no longer played, but talked to Kyo who leaned towards him over the piano top. Annette Rouleau looked after him coldly, then turned back to concentrate on the storm, hugging herself in terror.

A few feet away from Annette, Daniel stood at the window, flashing his torch out into the night. Its sinewy gleam fell on the muddy bog of the lawn, its surface rippled with the wind. Upturned garden furniture lay rocking about, legs in the air, stiff and white as dead animals. Bits of debris and uprooted shrubs charged the window of the lounge. The beam of the torch cut into the night, and illuminated faintly a wall at the end of the lawn. Beyond it waves rose and crashed, sometimes towering up upon the wall itself, stalking the fragile human world inside the Cooper's house.

Geraldine glanced at the window nervously as she directed the maid with the clearing up, then hurried into the kitchen.

'Now,' she said firmly, emerging again a few minutes later, her hands full of a roll of pink paper. 'Now we are going to play, pin the tail on the elephant. Yes, elephant, simply because I cannot draw a donkey. I can only draw an elephant. And here he is.' She held up before her a large shocking pink paper elephant. The children came towards her.

'He's rather good, don't you think? We can't pin him on the wall because they're concrete, we'll have him on the floor.' She spread the paper on the carpet and waved a stringy tail in the air, sitting back upon her heels. 'Come along, my poppets. Who shall we blindfold first?'

Arthur and Nate discussed typhoons, across the bamboo bar. Arthur sat sideways on his stool to keep an eye on Kyo, who talked to Dennis Denzel over the piano top. She was already drunk; he had seen her refill her glass several times at the bar when Nate was engaged with the candles. Dennis Denzel played up to her attention, bored with the uncle image he had portrayed since the children arrived.

'I wan' more whisky. You wan' more whisky Den'is? I get us some.' She pulled herself off the piano and turned unsteadily to Arthur and Nate at the bar.

'One more,' she said coquettishly, her head on one side. The red hair hung damp and stringy about her face, her eyes questioned pertly.

Arthur cleared his throat. 'I think you've had enough. Quite enough.'

The pertness turned to anger in Kyo's narrow eyes. 'You gimme some. Who are you to tell me no?' she flared, her voice thickly slurred.

'All right. All right. Just a little. We don't want to upset the lady, Arthur. This is not the time for a quarrel.' Nate poured a little whisky in her glass and filled it up with water.

'It's real weak,' he said quietly to Arthur.

'An' one for my friend.' Kyo indicated Dennis, who nodded to Nate from the piano stool. She swayed uncertainly back with the glasses to Dennis.

'Come on. Let's sit down over there. I wanna' talk with you. I like you. You're a nice man.' She led Dennis to an empty sofa the other side of the room. He grinned back to Nate and Arthur, an apologetic grin.

Arthur looked down into the amber well of his glass. He shook it absently, the ice clunked and knocked. He hated to see her like this. Kyo. He saw what she had become, but it made no difference to the feelings that stirred within him still. The wayward look in her slim dark eyes had only added to those hours they had shared so many years ago. Now that look had soured, hard as stone in her face. Yet still she drew him, and he suffered in the humiliation of her total disregard. He knew now for certain how little he had meant to her. Watching her on the sofa, playing up to Dennis Denzel, he wished as he had many times that evening, to take her and shake her. To tell her, it is I, Arthur. Arthur. But he knew there would be blankness in her eyes, until he reminded her of the circumstances of their encounters. And it would be that last time she remembered, not him. She would remember only the child, Akiko. Unable to look any longer he turned his back on her, and stared sadly at his glass, swirling the whisky over the ice. With an effort he attended to Nate Cooper, who was asking some question about the typhoon.

Eva was relieved to relinquish part of the evening to Geraldine, whose plump, upraised posterior could be seen across the lounge, showing glimpses of sturdy thigh, leading the screams of laughter as the elephant's tail was pinned to an eye. Eva sat in a chair near the bar and allowed Nate Cooper to give her a brandy. She sipped it slowly, and felt the coarse fire slip down into her. It seemed the night would never end. Soon they must get the children to sleep. Some were already bedded down in the lounge by Yoshiko and Eiko, and Yoshiko herself looked ready to collapse. But Eva could no longer apply fact to reality. Her feet did not seem to touch the ground, her body swam on through the night while she trailed some distance behind. She rested her head on her hand and watched Geraldine blindfold Mariko.

'She should've had kids,' Nate Cooper observed from the bar. 'All those committees, etcetera, etcetera, it's only surrogate motherhood.'

Eva gazed up at him, surprised and listened as Nate continued. 'We had a child once, a girl, Marianne. Died at six months from viral pneumonia. She wouldn't have any more after that, and I'm not much help. Business, business, nothing but business, or so Gerry tells me. What else can I do? I'm like that. The only thing I seem to know how to give her is money and more money. But that doesn't cure it all, does it?' He took a loud sip from his whisky, and his voice was slightly slurred when he spoke again. 'It's not been much good between us lately. Guess we're getting on, can't fool ourselves much longer. No, guess there's something ailing us. Seems to me we have a helluva lot going on around us, and nothing in the middle. I can see it tonight with your kids in here. It's giving us both a kick. Look at her there, she's loving it.' He paused and swallowed loudly, then called across to Geraldine.

'Hey, Gerry. That one over there, the fat one with the

plaster, what's his name, Hiroshi. He missed his turn. You've gotta play fair there now.' Nate Cooper left the bar, ambled over to Geraldine and proceeded to direct the game above his wife's plump form. Eva sat back and watched, appreciative and surprised at the Coopers' strengths and generosities. She had misjudged them as shallow people.

They were everything Eva had always rejected and avoided, the Kobe crowd, as she called the perennial, socially-orientated foreign expat community. For she herself had a life of great content and meaning, the kind of life not given to many of the foreigners who came to Japan. She knew herself used for a privileged purpose that broke down all barriers. But generally the luckless foreign resident remained entrenched in the mental cantonment the Japanese had reserved for them, back on the maps of 1870. Any puny efforts to supersede it were doomed before they began; Japanese society was a closed and impenetrable thing. And it was sad, Eva felt, that a clear human exchange between the races must be reduced to the rare event. She saw the faults on both sides for this, the mutual mistrust and ignorance. For the Japanese, the foreigner was forever the barbarian, an ugly, gormless, lolloping creature, filled with all the boundless spontaneity the Japanese had been taught to abhor from the beginning of time.

And the average foreign resident, experiencing sooner or later the reality of their position, refused to show patience or respect for the centuries of insulation that had produced this social system, more ordered and often more workable than their own. They condescended airily to what they considered quaint, esoteric and inscrutable, and returned quickly to their clique at the club, and the comfort of their own kind.

Eva had neither time nor patience for the attitudes of either side. There was work to be done, and she applied herself to it and found another plane to live upon. It was a long time since she had observed the Hartley Rovers and Annette Rouleaus of this world. She looked across at Dennis Denzel and noticed Kyo then.

She sat snuggled up to Dennis in the depths of a pale green sofa, her feet curled up beneath her. She rested an elbow on Dennis's shoulder, and played with a strand of his hair. He leaned back and listened to Kyo's chatter unravel about him like loose wool. Her tipsy attention was like the continuous buzzing of a tiresome bee, and he pulled his head away from her fingers, feeling he had had enough. Making an excuse, he heaved himself heavily to his feet, and turned back towards the bar. Kyo pulled at a handful of his shirt.

'Hey, where you going? You've not finished your drink. She tugged him back towards her and he tumbled onto the cushions.

'You can't leave Kyo alone,' she pouted. 'I told you I like you. And you like me too, don't you?'

'Yes, yes. But there is something I must ask Nate Cooper. Now, sit here like a good girl, I'll be back.' Dennis stood up and hurried off, relieved to have escaped.

'Don't leave Kyo alone,' she pouted again, speaking in a childish voice. 'I'm coming too. Anyway I wan' more whisky.' She stood unsteadily and Eva, watching her across the room, rose from her chair. She prayed Kyo would not disgrace them; she was already unbalanced and now she was drunk. She wondered how to handle her, but felt too tired to think.

Daniel burst in suddenly then with Jiro and Kenichi. They rushed across to the window. 'From what we can see, the sea-wall is down, the road is flooded. There's water all about the house, and the level seems to be rising. The boys have just shown me from an upstairs window.'

'The wall began to break a long time ago. We saw it earlier, when we took the candles up to Sister Elaine. We just went back now to have a look,' Jiro and Kenichi said together.

The room was filled with frightened voices, children began to whimper. Yoshiko sat down and started to cry and Eiko bent to her.

'I can't take any more,' sobbed Yoshiko. 'What will become of us all?'

'It can't last much longer,' comforted Eiko. 'Don't let the children see you like this.' Watching her the circle of small eyes absorbed her fear.

Geraldine's voice rose suddenly then from the kitchen. 'Nate. There's water in here, water.' She rushed into the lounge, her face torn open in panic. 'It's oozing in under the door, Nate.'

'It's coming under the front door, too,' Arthur Wilcox called from the entrance hall, where he had dashed at Geraldine's alert. For a moment there was silence, then everyone began to talk at once.

'Hart, Hart,' Annette's voice rose above them all, taut and thin. 'Hart, what shall we do? I can't take any more.' Annette shrank into a corner of the sofa, hugging herself in terror. At her feet Kimiko had woken. She began to cry, staring at Annette as she sucked her thumb.

'Pull yourself together Annette, you're upsetting the kids.' Hartley bent and picked up Kimiko, talking to her quietly.

'I can't, I'm ill. Ill, Hart. Do you hear? I've suddenly got awful pains. What'll become of us all?'

Emiko and Toshio had woken and were sobbing loudly. The older children looked at the faces of the adults with terrified expressions, more small ones began to cry. The women bent to comfort them. Eva took Kimiko from Hartley, and looked anxiously at Annette, who had started to shiver. Yoshiko composed herself quietly and turned to the children.

'Keep calm folks. How high can it rise? We simply go up stairs to a higher level. There's no need to panic. We shall be safe.' Nate Cooper spoke with assurance.

Outside, water sluiced triumphantly over the broken sea-wall no longer dividing ocean and road. The waves pounded forward unimpeded, and broke against the Coopers' wall, thrusting under their copper gates.

'We had none of this earlier,' Nate expressed private alarm to Arthur. 'The eye has passed, the winds are reversed. They are pulling the sea towards us now.' Arthur tugged at his moustache.

'God, when will it end?' Nate's face turned a streaky grey. A wet stain began on the carpet from the further corner of the lounge, spreading like a shadow.

'Up,' shrieked Geraldine. 'We must go up.' She pointed to the ceiling.

From the kitchen and hallway water oozed rapidly into the house. The garden was already submerged, a dark band of water bordered the window outside. Wind whipped up small waves upon what was once the lawn, shrubs floated like craft about the legs of the garden furniture. Large breakers crashed in waterfalls over the wall and rolled upon the window. One slammed itself upon the glass, enclosing them for a moment in a black wall of sea.

'Up. Up. Don't just stand there with wet feet, do something, Nate,' Geraldine cried again.

'I am neither Noah nor possess the Ark!' replied Nate. 'But up we must go without a doubt. Up, in fact to our eagle's nest. There we shall be safe.'

'Oh quickly, quickly,' urged Geraldine.

The children huddled in groups about the women.

Yoshiko's face appeared glazed. Children clutched at her skirt, sobbing. Eiko looked at her anxiously.

'Take some candles everyone, please. I've another box here,' Geraldine motioned them forward.

'Come on now, everyone, follow me.' Nate Cooper led them to the stairs.

Annette Rouleau still huddled on the sofa, moaning, 'Hartley, Hartley.'

'Get a hold on yourself, Annette. We're going upstairs, we'll be safe there. Come on.'

'I can't move. I've terrible pains,' Annette sobbed. 'Oh Hart, I'm so frightened.'

'Annette. Come on.'

'I can't.' Annette shook her head, her silver chains clinked. Taking hold of her arm Hartley pulled her to her feet. She gave little shrieks of agitation bending double as he dragged her forward. Another wave smashed upon the window, Annette screamed again. Behind her Junko started to cry and Eiko picked her up.

The children were assembled into a line. Arthur Wilcox took the blind child, Ruriko, Dennis Denzel carried Toshio and held Tami by the hand. Beside him Kyo swayed unsteadily.

'Come on. Follow me.' Nate Cooper led the way. 'You kids want to know how an eagle feels in his nest at the top of the tree? Well, you'll soon find out.' Nate Cooper made an effort to speak calmly over his shoulder to the crowd of frightened children.

'I don't want to climb a tree,' Emiko sobbed, stopping in her tracks.

'Don't like eagles,' Jun's lip trembled.

'Peck you to death,' Takeo said in a high, tight voice.

Yumiko and Mariko clutched each other. Yoshiko, alarmed, put an arm about Emiko.

'No, no. It's a room. We call it our eagle's nest because it's on top of the house. It's our den, our hidy-hole. Real high. We don't use all this when we're alone.' Nate gestured to the rooms below as he climbed the stairs.

They trooped up past the mezzanine and bedroom levels and took another flight of stairs. Their candles blew giant shadows on the walls and the children watched them fearfully, their sobs mixed with the shuffle of feet.

'We place ourselves in thy hands, O Lord,' Eva prayed as she climbed. Upon her shoulder Kimiko slept.

Hartley Rover steered Annette firmly by the arm. She gave little cries under her breath. Suddenly she doubled up, collapsing on the stairs. Behind her Dennis Denzel lurched to a stop, Toshio in his arms. He changed his candle to the other hand, his thumb enbalmed with wax.

'Get up. Come on,' Hartley said impatiently. Annette nursed her stomach.

'I can't, I'm ill. I'm in pain. Hartley, help me.'

'It's nerves, Annette, get up, you're worse than a child. None of these kids are behaving like you.' He wished for a way to escape, but the crocodile of bodies packed him tight against the banisters.

'You brought any whisky with you Den'is?' Kyo pawed Dennis Denzel, who was hung about uncomfortably with a child and candle.

'Shut up,' hissed Dennis, changing Toshio's weight and his candle to the other arm again. Toshio gave a shudder and started to sob, and immediately Tami looked anxiously up at him, and began to cry herself.

'There, there. It'll be all right,' the encumbered Dennis reassured the children. Kyo pulled at his arm again and his candle flickered.

'What about I go back for the whisky, Den'is? Then we can be cosy.'

'You get up these stairs.' Dennis turned upon her. Toshio and the candle tilted dangerously, their black shadows stretching elastically up the wall.

'Maybe you not such a nice man,' Kyo said sullenly.

'Come on, Annette.' Hartley pulled her forward brusquely. Annette trod on her caftan. There was the thin tear of silk and she gave a little scream.

'I hate you, Hartley Rover. I hate you.'

'Just now the feeling's mutual, Annette. But for the moment we must get up these stairs, we must get through the night.' He gave her another rough tug.

'Welcome to our hidy-hole.' Nate Cooper threw open the door before them.

The candles illuminated a room of mostly glass. The sun roof was sloped like an attic ceiling and from its concrete struts baskets of fern hung prettily. Two potted lemon trees stood in a corner. There were large deep sofas in an Eastern patterned print, scatter rugs and cushions were strewn about the floor. It was a pleasant room on a happier day. Now the glass roof drummed deafeningly with rain and took the rap of the storm as the room stood up, exposed, like a periscope above the house.

'It's noisy but safe, I promise you. That glass is strong as steel.' Nate smiled reassuringly, but Annette was unconvinced and began to cry again. Under the thunderous rattle of the storm the children stood mute and stiff with fear. Beneath the glass roof, hanging baskets of fern swung gently in vibration.

'We'll be safe up here.' Nate Cooper smiled broadly.

'Oh, and if it were nicer weather I could show you the sauna, just across from this room on the roof. Nate brought it from Finland last year. It's a little gem, I couldn't live without it,' Geraldine enthused, feeling immediately better at this higher level. The children stared at her petrified, choking back sobs.

'I want the bathroom.' Junko pressed her knees together, her breath small rasps of fear. Eva hurried her from the room. Nobuo ran after her, another two followed him.

At the window Arthur Wilcox stared out into the night. 'Good God, come and look at this,' he called to Nate. Everyone hurried forward.

The churning mass of water had flooded the road and neighbouring homes. Beside the house the river boiled down from higher land to the right of the Coopers' house, only their high wall contained its swollen overflow. The last few feet of the submerged garden wall squared off a field of water within a larger expanse of sea. And still the waves continued to break, great surfing spills of foam, smashing over the Coopers' wall, rolling on towards the house to fling themselves upon it. An unexpected streak of lightning cut the sky open and illuminated the whole disaster. Beyond what was once the sea wall two boats, broken from their moorings, pitched about. Much further out on the bay were the lights of anchored ships, rolling and tossing.

'Don't look,' Eva commanded, coming back into the room with Junko and Nobuo. She hurried the children away from the window. 'It'll soon be finished, it cannot go on much longer. We shall be safe up here. We must try and get some rest now.' Before her the children nodded, overcome by the night's experience. About them the room flickered in candlelight, rain flailed on the glass roof, the noise resounding in their ears. They choked back sobs and looked at Eva.

Annette Rouleau's hysteria still dominated the room. Hartley carried her to a nearby sofa and arranged her there.

'Are your tranquillisers in this bag, Annette?' Hartley fumbled in Annette's lizard skin handbag for her silver pillbox and pressed a tablet between her lips.

'Swallow it,' he commanded. 'And now lie quiet.'

'It's just nerves,' Eva said quietly to Hartley, coming up beside him. She bent to Annette.

'Try and relax, my dear. It will soon be over. We shall be all right. Try taking deep breaths.'

Annette Rouleau looked at her weakly, and started to sob again. Eva patted her arm and turned to Geraldine.

'We must bed these poor children down somehow. They cannot take any more.'

'I'll fetch up some pillows and blankets,' Geraldine offered quickly. Eva nodded and went with her to help.

6

She had had the most wonderful dream. She and Horace had been at a croquet match at Mrs de Bainville's. They were sitting with glasses of iced lemonade in a charming white summerhouse. Beyond the windows the lawn stretched lime and acid under the sun, spread with croquet hoops. There was the gentle knock of the ball, the sounds of voices and laughter. Lettice Banebridge and Evangeline Simmons had suddenly appeared with the treat of bowls of strawberries. Lettice wore a floppy white hat with a tulle bird upon it. As Maud watched the bird grew real and took flight, fluttering about the walls of the summerhouse. Horace jumped up and soon caught it, but he did not give it back to Lettice. He came towards Maud, cupping the bird in his hands. His eyes were smiling down at her, deep blue and crinkled at the corners. She felt the soft warmth of the bird in her hand, the frightened beat of its heart. Then she had woken, the dream breaking softly in her head, until only Horace's eyes remained with her. Horace's eyes. She smiled to herself in the candlelight.

Somewhere behind there must have been another dream, for she had also the memory of meeting young Arthur Wilcox. They had talked of many things and time had dissolved. She told him, she remembered, about the balloon ascent, and there was something too about Rudyard Kipling of all people.

Outside the storm still raged. She could hear the beastly thing crashing and banging about. The sleep had done her good, she felt animated. Everything seemed melted and stirred, as if the past was the present and the present of no regard. And what did it matter if it were? It was only her memories that kept her alive. She remembered then again the nasty shock she had received that morning, or was it yesterday? When Geraldine had appeared so suddenly in Mama's red velvet dress. Just remembering the anger surged up in her once more, shattering the gentle dreams. Mama had given the dress to her, and Maud had kept it safe for years in a silk-lined trunk. What right had Geraldine to take it? What right? Maud Bingham struggled to sit up in bed, to feel her anger the better. It descended to her knees. She remembered the red shelf that was Geraldine's belly below the nip of whalebones. Horrid, horrid, horrid.

It was all choking in her throat now, the dead events of which she had only the ash of memory, that came and went as they pleased. It was more than she could bear, she must do something to stop it, to show them she was not a heap of old bone. She was as real as each of her memories. And it came to her then, just slipped whole and cool into her mind. She knew what she would do, her head sang with it. And Mama most certainly would have approved.

When her feet touched the floor she felt weak and giddy with excitement. She sat back on the bed to steady herself. About her shadows moved across the walls behind the candle's small bright eye. The deep black corners of the room were like the pockets of the past, unending, full of density and substance. What right had Geraldine? What right? The carpet was soft and supportive under her feet. She went very slowly, moving one leg after the other. She thought, they told me I couldn't walk. Or was it that she should not? But it did not matter. She had deceived them. She reached for the handle of the door. Its knob was smooth beneath her hand, opening quietly. And suddenly she wanted to laugh out loud, for she knew there was nothing she could not do.

It was Geraldine's room she must go to. She concentrated on her legs, pushing them one before the other. Her hands felt their way along the wall. Geraldine's door was before her now, and opened noiselessly. Here, too, a candle had been lighted. The room flickered about her. Maud walked forward; she knew what she must do.

She found Geraldine's walk-in closet easily. And in it the dress, almost the first one she touched. She knew it in spite of the darkness, she knew the sleek cold touch of the velvet, held in her mind since childhood. She knew it at once in the darkness, hanging limp and lifeless in Geraldine's closet, like a wretched misjudged soul. 'Poor thing,' she said, and took it from the hanger.

Before the mirror, in the candlelight, she held it to herself. And saw again the fur circular and muff Mama had some-times worn with the dress. The thick folds of the gown gleamed lustrously in the soft light. On the dressing table the little flame of the candle flickered, the dim room drew close about Maud Bingham. But her heart began suddenly to pound, and she gripped the dress tightly to her body, for she saw in the mirror a ghost. It could be nothing else. The creature stood skeletal and pale, the bones of the face shredded cadaverously by candlelight, thin white hair askew on its balding skull. Maud Bingham backed away, but the ghost moved only slightly, standing its ground. And she saw then that it was herself she gazed at. The shock made her tremble all over.

Slowly, she unhooked the dress, her fingers shaking. Sitting on Geraldine's bed she lifted each foot into the skirt and, her gums chattering with excitement, pulled the gown over her thick pink nightdress, and stuck her arms into each velvet sleeve. She heaved the weight of it onto her shoulders, and stood before the mirror again. 'Oh Mama,' she said.

And waved in her hand an imaginary fan, just as Mama might have done. A little fan of feathers and sequins, like the one Mama had often fluttered prettily.

'Mother ... Mother ... Mother ...' She stopped, her head reeling from her thoughts. She knew that voice, it was Geraldine. Nearly stumbling in the long thick folds of the dress, she hurried to the closet again, pulling the door behind her.

'Mother ... Mother ... Mother ...' Geraldine's voice was in the room, outside the closet.

Maud held her breath, standing still between the hangers. The soft touch of silk and cotton folded close about her. There were stale smells from the armpits of a dress hanging against her nose. On a shelf above, the small cold claws of a limp fox collar dangled on her neck. She feared she might sneeze. Outside she heard the rush of movement and the shriek of Geraldine's voice again.

The clothes blew softly back upon her and hid her as Geraldine pulled open the door and stuck her head inside the closet, then shut it again with a bang. On her neck the claws of the fox moved and scratched her gently. Maud Bingham was delighted she had evaded her daughter.

She giggled and pulled from the shelf above the fur collar, wrapped it around her neck and groped again on the shelf. She found a wide-brimmed hat and tugged it down firmly upon her head. Then she waited for a while, listening, before carefully opening the closet door.

The squat stub of a candle still burned in the room and she picked it up as she passed. Her hip was stiff, she hobbled painfully now. But the room was quieter, the wind seemed to have dropped and no longer charged the house. The night appeared more orderly, a low mewling sound outside was all she could hear. She felt suddenly weak and giddy with tiredness, and sat on Geraldine's bed to rest. But the thought was strong in her still, she would deceive them. It was like a window in her mind, opening out, and her heart palpitated with excitement. She made her way to the door; the smell of mothballs drifted up from her dress as she moved.

Passing the stairs to Nate Cooper's den, she heard sounds of voices and shuffled on as fast as she could. They had not found her. The thought sang in her head and she hugged herself in glee and pulled the wide black hat more firmly down upon her head. The corridor led her forward, shadowy and dim. The bodice of the dress fell off her shoulders and she hauled it back up again. There was a door to her right, and stopping, she opened it. The room was small and without any light. Her candle cracked the dark as she entered and fell on the turgid texture of a modern print hanging on the wall. But then her mouth quivered, for she saw the glass door across the room. Picking up her long skirt she hobbled towards it then stopped, a faintness washing through her. She gripped the brass rail of a bedstead and sat on the edge of the mattress. She must rest before she did anything else, for all her activities had tired her out. She lay down, settled her head on the pillow, and immediately fell asleep.

7

The noise of the storm drummed in Akiko's head, until she felt she could bear it no longer. Her nerves were frayed as torn linen. The room, the noise, the crush of tired people and crying children, and her own small shattered world, crowded down upon her. She could not cope, her throat filled with tears, she wanted to be alone with Daniel. She felt like a piece of flotsam, pitched helplessly upon the events of the day.

'Please, for a while come and sit with me,' she whispered, standing beside him at the window. The night still pummelled the glass before her; she was numb with it all. He turned and saw the stress in her face.

'Yes, come.' He put a hand on her arm. 'Let's go down to the landing.'

He guided her from the room. On the steps outside they peered down the stairwell, and saw by the light of their candle, the movement of water at the bottom of the stairs. A soft lapping noise came up to them.

'It's really filled up down there,' Daniel said.

On the upper landing they found a stout orange sofa, whose round bolstered shape reminded Akiko of Geraldine. When they sat down he put an arm round her.

'I don't want to talk. I just want to sit with you here, like this,' she told him, and leaned back upon his shoulder. A candle glowed on a Korean chest beside the sofa, its brasswork butterflies and hinges glimmered in the dark. The plaited strips of the parquet flooring stretched away across the landing.

'You can see by tonight how little you can expect to regulate life, and yet how much you can survive,' Daniel sighed.

In the glass of a print on the opposite wall they observed their own reflection, measuring themselves against the night and before the future under the flickering candlelight. The house was empty and quiet here, the storm removed from them. They sat in their separate silences, linked by their arms and the unfinished situations that lay folded and passive within them still. The pictureglass across the landing reflected them like a crystal ball, caught and paired together and already compliant within its walnut frame.

'When I go back to America, you shall come with me,' Daniel said. 'I shall not let you go now that I have found you. And you will be happy there. You will be welcomed.'

There was the smell of floor polish, and the smell of candles, and the briny flood downstairs. The odours rose up through the dark well of the house, a yeasty thickened smell. She knew she would remember it always as the forking of her life. Many times she had touched darkness for a sign but found only emptiness, dry and unexpressed. Now a new direction was taking shape. She listened to the slap of trapped water at the bottom of the house. There was nothing she could say. She wanted no more than Daniel. As she rubbed her cheek against his hand and closed her eyes upon his shoulder, Geraldine's scream sounded through the house.

'Mother. Mother. Nate, Mother's gone. She's not in her room or anywhere.' Geraldine appeared from the door of Maud Bingham's room.

'What do you mean, she's gone?' Nate yelled. 'Where could she get to, an old bone like that?' The stairs shook as he descended. Arthur followed after him.

Akiko and Daniel rushed with them into Maud Bingham's

room. The bed stood square and empty. Arthur bent immediately and looked beneath.

'I've looked everywhere. Everywhere,' Geraldine cried.

'Perhaps she's gone to the bathroom,' suggested Eva, appearing with her arms full of blankets.

'I told you I've looked everywhere.' Geraldine was hysterical.

'Can she walk alone?' Eva asked.

'A bit. I get her up a few hours in the day, for her circulation. But she can't hobble far, I'm sure.' Geraldine's eyes brimmed and overflowed, mascara ran in black tributaries.

'Where the hell is she, then?' Nate exploded. 'How many times must I tell you, Gerry, to go when the old girl calls?'

'She couldn't have gone down. Oh Nate. She couldn't have gone down now, could she?' Geraldine sobbed.

'I was with her as you know. And not so long ago either. When I left she was asleep,' Arthur reassured.

'We had best all start looking,' Daniel suggested and Nate nodded while Geraldine sobbed on Eva's shoulder.

'Half the time the old girl lives in the past. She's getting too much for Gerry,' Nate told them.

'Could she really have wandered downstairs?' Daniel asked.

'Can't walk far by herself. She broke a hip sitting down in a chair a few years ago. She can't get far. Damn miracle if she did. God, I need a whisky. What a night.'

'I'll get a torch from upstairs, we'll go down and look for her, and the whisky,' Daniel offered. Nate Cooper nodded, and turned to the sobbing Geraldine.

'We're going down, Gerry. We're going to look for the old girl.' In agitation Nate swished back the curtains of the window. He stared glumly at the black face of the glass and beyond it into the night. There violence continued to snarl at him. In the background Geraldine sobbed. Nate watched the waves bang down on the garden wall, burying his estate in explosions of spume. Then his face sharpened suddenly, he took a step forward and squared himself with the window.

'What's that?' he said to Daniel, who had returned with the torch.

'What?'

'That. Off the horizon there, don't you see it? That white line.' Nate pointed.

They strained their eyes at the window. The women and Arthur rushed forward. They could see it growing as they watched, a long thin finger of white across the bay, growing thicker and nearer, stretching as far as they could see. They watched it curiously, unable to decide.

'What is it, what is it? Oh Nate,' screeched Geraldine.

'Will you quit the hysterics, honey. We're trying to decide what it is. Dan and I here are breaking our brains, aren't we, kid?'

The line of white was constant and steady, thickening fast. They pressed their faces to the black vibrating glass. A great dyke of foam was rolling and hammering towards them out of the black wild night and the sea.

'Good God. Holy mackerel. It's a tidal wave.' Nate breathed the words in condensation onto the window glass.

Daniel and Akiko drew a sharp breath. Geraldine screamed and was helped to a chair by Eva. Arthur Wilcox began to dance on his toes.

'No. Not a tidal wave, a storm surge. A storm surge. A sudden tide against the coast. It can raise up the level of the sea by as much as three metres, in moments,' Arthur shouted.

'Good God,' gasped Nate.

'What can we do?' Daniel asked.

'Nothing, lad. Nothing,' said Arthur.

And then, at that moment, from downstairs they heard the sudden sound of singing. A drunken, slurred, unintelligible song, the high notes cracking and shrieking out in a terrible, grinding rhythm.

Arthur Wilcox fled the room, the others followed.

8

Coming down the stairs they descended into the splintered singing of Kyo's drunken voice. It swelled and multiplied, as caressing as a cactus limb. The voice curled through Akiko's body, sounding shameful and grotesque.

Daniel's torch wheeled about in the darkness, slicing open the black wet mess of the ground floor. They stood on the last stair and stepped down into ankle-deep water. It moved about them in an ugly way, washing against walls with a restless slap. They splashed across to the lounge and stood in the doorway, staring without a word.

'You get her, quick as you can, kid. I'll search out old Maud. When that wave hits, the whole flood will rise.' Nate Cooper hurried off to prospect for Maud Bingham.

Akiko stared and knew she would never again see anything so terrible. Shame pulsed hotly through her, and she lowered her eyes. Before them in the room the stubs of three candles still lived, faltering sometimes in invisible draughts. The piano rose like an island out of the flood, reflecting the gleam of the candle flames; upon it stood Kyo, hopelessly drunk.

She swayed and staggered on the piano top in the motions of some bawdy dance, gyrating in randy movements before an invisible audience. Once she stopped, picked up the bottle near her feet and took a lusty swig. Then she was off again.

'She must have come back down for the whisky. I had begun to wonder where she had gone,' said Arthur from behind Akiko.

'Kyo,' Daniel shouted, but the woman took no notice. He drew a breath and waded into the room. Akiko followed, her mind numb. Before her the spindly limbs upon the piano jerked like a puppet's on a string. The shredded sounds of the ribald song pressed inside her head. She remembered the words again then, and closed her eyes upon her own abasement. *Akiko, sometimes I like to hope you think of me. Mother.* The words melted with her shame. She could not believe only hours before she had handled them wonderingly, like precious glass. None of it seemed possible in the sequence of one day. She reached out and held tight to Daniel's hand. Behind them Arthur Wilcox flashed a torch about. His voice sprang up suddenly, yelling loudly in their ears, mixed with terrified screams from upstairs.

'The surge. The surge.' Arthur focused his torch on the window.

It happened in moments, there was no time to move. They looked together at the window and saw the black shelf of water, blacker than the sky, hovering and trembling as if to crash, yet standing, growing, advancing each moment, bearing down upon them. It rose to great height, a flourish of foam riding its summit, a final wrath released from the belly of the storm. It swallowed the garden wall, sucked it into itself without a break and came on towards the house. They saw then, carried upon its crest, a fishing boat ripped from its moorings, pitched about like a paltry toy.

Then the moment exploded. Glass was breaking and flying. Kyo was swept into the foaming water and mangled there. The split second unrolled like a slow motion film, stamped forever in Akiko's mind. She saw the loose slump of Kyo's body slung backwards by the roll of foam, slices and fragments of glass fly about and the great dark underside of the boat, thrust in through the window, riding up upon the piano as Kyo was thrown into the water. Her limbs flung about there, red strings of hair flashed in the froth as she was hurled against the piano again. A bloody slash opened up her head.

Akiko screamed. Then the world boiled about her like a thing possessed, a mountain of water poured into the lounge, whipping her backwards, tossing her head over heels. The raging weight of it hammered upon her. The world was at once white and unbridled, green-veined and marbled, black as slate and iron. Her lungs filled, she was choking and drowning, the savagery ripping her limbs from her body. Her lungs burst and gushed. Then there was blackness.

Again there was the green depth of water about Daniel, but this water, murky and dark, was pummelling and roaring about him. It was not the glassy underworld in which he had released himself from the car, deep beneath the river. Released himself into guilt and regret. Some terrible watery revenge was being beaten out upon him, and it was everything he deserved, everything. He remembered how he had pulled and pulled helplessly at Casey's body, unable to move it in the car. He remembered how he had manoeuvred himself through the open window. This was retribution, what he had waited for and knew would happen. He did not resist it, but accepted what must be. No other thought filled his head. Water gushed into his lungs, into his mouth and nose. Casey, he thought. Casey. It's what I deserve.

The water foamed, gnashing, hard as stone. Then he heard Akiko scream beside him and saw a tumble of limbs, saw her break the surface as he, too, was thrown up, only to be tossed under again.

'Akiko.' The water separated him from her.

'Akiko,' he yelled, and grabbed her as the water hurled her up. He pulled her to him, holding her tightly. They were out of their depth, he could not feel the floor, but the water no longer poured in with such force. He struck out, thrusting and pushing with his legs, battling with it all.

'It's all right. It's all right. We'll make it,' he shouted in Akiko's ear, swimming towards the stairs.

And in the midst of the clamour his mind suddenly opened, for his purpose in the night was clear to him now. It was retribution, retribution that would cut him down, unless he could pass through its slender eye, unless he could return a life for the life he had been unable to save. He thought of the night behind him, each segment of the disaster, each fragile escape, and found for himself a pattern in its mad tapestry. Found the fragments he must fit together to turn the night upon itself. Through it all the expectation of life had been infused with the expectation of death, equally divided. Each time at his side life had reassembled itself, shrugging off death. His mind was clear now, and he braced himself against the water. This was the last time, he knew.

'We'll make it, Casey.' He said the words over and over again, willing them through him and out of his body into the swelling water.

'Make it ... Casey ...'

They were under the open archway that led from the lounge to the entrance hall. He saw the stairs from the corner of his eye.

'Casey ... Casey ...' He willed the words again.

The floor was under him, and then the stairs. He pulled Akiko after him from the water. They lay like drowned rats on the steps. Daniel's body was heavy, and inert, but his head smarted with relief. It was over. He had done it. Done it.

'Casey,' he said, and touched the girl beside him.

From upstairs he heard, far away, the frightened crying of the children. And the faint note through it all of Hiroshi's voice repeating insistently.

'Toshio's wet himself.'

9

At the moment he saw the surge descending, Arthur Wilcox retreated quickly some way up the stairs. His heart jumped about like a stone in his chest. In the candlelight he saw a great mountain of foam hit the window, and within it the prow of the boat, driving down upon the house. Then the night split upon an immense noise as the glass was blasted to smithereens in a savage spasm of water. Huge and dark, the prow of the boat drove into the lounge flinging Kyo from the piano like a pile of matchsticks. He heard her scream. Her limbs thrashed about in the torrent, disappearing, thrown upwards, and disappearing again. Water swirled up about Arthur. He grabbed the banisters, the room was suddenly dark, the sea gushed about him, he smelled its strong rank smell. Flashing his torch about he strained his eyes into the turmoil before him.

'Kyo.' The word tore out of him.

Kyo. It burst in him, dissolving time. At that moment in a single image he saw his life, in the calcified smile of Maud Bingham's old teeth suspended, inane and futile, in a glass beside her bed.

Kyo.

He plunged in. The water hit him, cold and angry, full of yeasty curdle. He struck out firmly, and found the water easing, the great wave over, the spume settling like scum upon the swelling surface. He made out in the darkness Daniel, swimming, dragging with him the girl, Akiko.

'Kyo.' He spluttered the word into the water. She did not answer, just floated there before him. In the darkness he made out only the pale aqueous form of her face. He clutched at her, pulling her to him. His hands felt the coarse strands of her wet hair. Holding her firmly he started swimming slowly back towards the stairs. The water pushed against him buoyantly. Someone was shining a torch; a point of light danced about him. He saw a crystallised plum on a paper plate float past on a sudden swell. Cigarette butts and chocolate wrappers, cream crackers and a beer can rose on the murky tide. Arthur pushed it all aside. He could feel the floor beneath him now; he stood up and dragged Kyo from the water. Nate Cooper put down his torch and helped pull her onto the safety of the stairs.

'Oh God,' said Nate. He bent to shake Daniel and Akiko, slumped on the steps above them. 'You kids okay?'

'There's a boat in your lounge. It rammed the glass in that surge,' said Arthur, kneeling to Kyo.

'God,' Nate Cooper repeated.

Akiko opened her eyes. Against her was the hard awkward shape of the stairs, cutting under her neck. Her head ached and thumped, and she felt nauseous. In the dimness she saw Daniel's head beside her. He stirred as she watched and raised his face, his hair sodden and dripping over his brow.

'Are you all right?' he asked. She nodded, and tried to sit up. Her head swam.

'We had quite a ducking there. Thank God I got hold of you.' He put out a hand and gripped her wrist. 'I'll never let you escape me, you'll see.'

There was torchlight from above, and behind it appeared Eva, Dennis and Hartley, all relieved at the sight of the group on the stairs.

'Thank the Lord. I hardly dare come and look.' Eva sat down on a step and bending put her arms about the wet Akiko.

'Are you all right? We were all terrified.'

'We've got a boat in the lounge,' Nate shouted up to Dennis and Hartley.

'The eye of the fleet, no doubt,' joked Dennis. Nate gave a half-hearted laugh.

'What happened up there? Gerry and the kids okay?' he asked.

'Yes. Your windows stood up to it all. Nothing broke. We just had a scare. What a scare. Those poor kids are terrified, they'll never get over tonight. And Annette's a goner. She's worse than the kids,' Hartley told them.

Nate Cooper picked up the torch Arthur Wilcox had placed

upon a stair and swung it about the wet tatters of his home. The sound of the flood made soft lapping noises about the clumps of stoic furniture that awaited fate in silent dignity, like overstuffed matrons, straight-faced through a risque joke. A few paper plates, left by the orphans upon the table, now floated as the pale flat leaves of lotus would upon a night-time lake. Nate Cooper groaned to himself again.

'Dr Kraig,' Arthur called out in an anxious voice. He had Kyo laid out flat on her stomach across an extra wide step of the stairs. Eva came down to him.

'I've been trying to give her some artificial respiration, but there is no response. She went under the water, and as you can see, cut her head too,' Arthur said worriedly. Eva bent down to Kyo, turning her over, picking up a limp wet hand.

'She's dead,' she whispered. 'Quite dead.'

The words broke in Akiko, filling her mind. The feeling swelled and bloomed and burst, pushing for release. She began to sob, great scoops of sound leaving her in an obsessive rhythm, unstoppable. And each sound was a rent in the past.

Akiko, sometimes I like to hope you think of me. She hacked it to bits with her cries.

Mother. Mother. The word was stretched tighter than skin on a drum. It shattered within her to fragments.

The black watery grave of the house, the grey dim ceilings and stairs above, the brown murky sea below; all pressed up in a dark passage through her. It was the night, it was the past, and all the future still held and had lost. Her body trembled with some terrible, shapeless thing that was neither hatred nor love.

'Mother.' She sobbed it out at last, staring down at the silent form on the steps below, staring at her mother. Kyo's hand lay, palm upwards on the wet carpet, her fingers cupped in an empty shape.

'Mother.' And again and again. Cutting it loose from her flesh.

Then Daniel was there, shaking her gently. 'Akiko.'

Her tears were free and easy now.

'It's over.' Daniel turned her away.

10

She did not open the door immediately. She had lain down on the bed in the room for a rest, for all the activities had tired her out. Maud Bingham sat up and rubbed her eyes, feeling much better. The candle still burned on the chest of drawers, where she had placed it when she came in. Slowly she got off the bed, and her mind was at once full of it all again. They had no idea where she was. She remembered Geraldine's voice again, calling desperately. Mother ... Mother... Maud Bingham giggled. There did not seem as much noise now outside, the wind appeared to have abated. In the room the candle flickered and gleamed on mahogany gloss.

'Horace,' she said, for she thought she saw him standing there, but when she looked there was nothing. Just the curve of the old whatnot that had once belonged to her mother. She had given it to Geraldine as a wedding present. Horace had been most upset at the pale silhouette left on the wall after it went. He insisted they redecorate immediately.

And she remembered then. Of course, Horace would be in the garden, pruning the roses. She hobbled to the glass door that led onto the balcony, and pushed her frail weight against it. Outside the wind was cool and blew hard upon her. It ripped the hat from her head immediately and sent it spinning into the air, spinning and spinning.

The balcony was long and appeared to stretch around the house. She took a step forward, hesitant in the dark, and trod on the skirt of her dress. It pulled off her shoulders again, rain slapped lightly about her face.

'A little rain will be good for the roses, Horace.' She held onto the rail of the balcony. The fur ruffled at her neck, its hair blew into her mouth.

'Horace.' She pulled herself along the balcony. Her mind was a honeycomb in which thoughts and pictures buzzed in and out like a swarm of bees. She stopped, holding her head between her hands, for suddenly it ached and rang with confusion. She could not remember why she stood here, why she must deceive them, and who were *they*. Why was Horace not here beside her? Why must he prune roses in the dark, and where was she anyway? There was a lake below the balcony, stretching out as far as she could see, without beginning or end. Like the great lake Biwa near Kyoto, where she and Horace had sometimes stayed. She remembered the large wood-beamed hotel, and tea on the lawns at the edge of the lake. Horace had always enjoyed the boating. She recalled him helping her into a boat from the landing stage near the lawn.

'Horace.' For she saw him at last. There again on the lake in the boat. She leaned over the balcony and she could see him quite clearly below, smiling, stretching his arm up to help her down.

She leaned further out to grasp his hand. She must reach it, she must get to him. Then the buzzing in her head would stop. And there was this feeling that she must get away, must get to Horace, where no one could touch her. Only there would she be entirely free.

'Horace. Horace.' She felt the touch of his fingertips.

But she was falling. Falling. The wind rushed about her, blowing the musty old fox into her mouth again.

'Horace. Horace.'

But it did not matter, for she knew he would catch her. Already she saw him open his arms.

'Horace.'

11

In Nate Cooper's hidy-hole the bodies of sleeping children covered the floor. The adults sat about, some dozing fitfully, others unable to sleep shifted positions restlessly, or talked quietly together. The candles had burnt to stumps but still filled the room with a warm light, the walls moved with shadows. The flames of the candles reflected small bright eyes on the glass sun-roof but the blinds were drawn at the windows, the night was shut away. They had all relaxed, the typhoon was dying. Outside the wind was a low and melancholy sound, moaning its own sudden death. The storm had passed. In the Coopers' hidy-hole they waited for the morning.

In their bedroom on the floor below, Geraldine Cooper sobbed and sobbed.

'Mother. Mother. Oh Nate. Poor Mother.'

'I know, honey. I know.' Nate Cooper comforted her as best he could. 'We'll find her in the morning, honey. There is no way we can dredge downstairs now. No way.'

In his mind he began the task of totting up the expense of all the damage. He would have liked to get out his calculator. But he decided it might be best to wait until Geraldine stopped her sobbing. It could not be long.

12. Saturday

They found Maud Bingham in the morning, face down in the slushy remains of the flood. With the turn of the tide the sea retreated, leaving behind ankle-deep watery mud. People emerged and were seen in rubber boots, inspecting the state of their properties. Large patches of sea were still trapped upon land and lay like pieces of jigsaw, brimming with the sky. Within them the passage of clouds was recorded. The day was washed and cool, its colours sharp and damp and delicate, restored anew.

In the Coopers' garden the lawn was still water-logged behind the broken wall. The bulk of a large green and white boat was wedged half in and half out of a patio window. Its splintered keel was encrusted with barnacles, its hatch smashed against the top of the window, a fishing net trailing over its side. In the bedraggled, swampy lounge its bows rode high upon the grand piano, a dark and grotesque intrusion.

Maud Bingham lay outside on the lawn, in a foot of gravy-coloured water, her body sodden with mud. The red velvet gown and below it her nightdress made an emulsified blanket about her. The fox at her neck was a slimy rope. A hat of black satin taffeta was retrieved floating near the wall. But under the mud caking Maud Bingham's skin there appeared to be a gentle smile. They carried her to the porch.

'Oh Mother ... Poor Mother.' Geraldine Cooper fell on her knees and took her mother's head upon her lap, rocking it there like a child. Standing near her Nate Cooper observed the filthy gown, the fox, and the hat placed beside Maud Bingham.

'Don't grieve so, honey. It had to be some time. Looks to me like the old girl deceived us all and took off in a grand old fling. I reckon she went as she wanted to.' Nate Cooper spoke with an air of detachment to the serenity of the morning.

'Oh, you unfeeling man. How can you say such things?' Geraldine glared with reddened eyes, and looked back in distress at her mother and the remains of the centenary dress.

But already her mind was absorbing the shock and extending itself to rituals. The hat had been her black funeral hat. A replacement would have to be quickly bought. The dress, though, was an irreplaceable loss, and it was doubtful if it would dry clean. But if it did not, thought Geraldine, there should be no problem in taking a pattern to make a replica of the gown. And then pulled herself up sharply, shocked to find such thoughts in her mind before her mother's body. Tears filled her eyes again.

From the window of the bedroom Eva watched the ambulance draw up at the gates. It had come for Sister Elaine; she turned to the bed and smiled. Early that morning the police had been out scouring the neighbourhood, assessing the damage. They found the wreck of the orphanage and worried, came looking for Eva and the children. They soon found them at the Coopers', and sent a man back to the main police station in Kobe to send word to the orphanage in Osaka, and to the hospital for Sister Elaine. The ambulance had not taken long to arrive. The policeman returned with a message that the orphanage bus had left from Osaka, to take the children back there.

'The ambulance is here. Now you'll soon feel more comfortable. Later today, when I get to Osaka, I intend to speak to the Mother Superior. I shall suggest a long holiday to convalesce. You should return for a while to Ireland, I think.'

'But not for too long,' urged Sister Elaine. 'I do want to be back for the Christmas events. I have decided to make a new Christmas manger with the children.'

'I doubt if we shall be in our own home this year. The damage is terrible. There was a landslide too, a great sea of mud was washed into the house, and more trees came down. What a narrow escape we had. The damage sounds much too bad to go back. No, I should think they will hurry through the last phases of the plans and start instead with the new building. In the meanwhile we shall have to move to Osaka. A bus is already on its way for us all from there,' Eva told Sister Elaine.

'It has been the most terrible night. And yet not without great purpose for me. The ways of the Lord are indeed strange. But I shall be all right now, Dr Kraig, I know it.' Sister Elaine sighed peacefully.

Two men with a stretcher entered the room, behind them Jiro and Kenichi and several other children. They were still dressed in Geraldine's bright sweaters and crowded round the bed.

'Mrs Cooper gave us paper and pencils. We made you get well cards to take to the hospital.' Kenichi pushed himself forward to take charge of the proceedings.

'There wasn't enough paper for us all, so several of us made each card and signed it.' He thrust the pile into her hands.

'Well, if that wasn't just what I needed to get me better,' smiled Sister Elaine.

'Will you be back soon?' Jiro asked.

'I really don't know at this moment. But I shall try.'

'We'll write,' Kenichi promised for them all. The others nodded behind him.

The men lifted Sister Elaine onto the stretcher and folded a blanket about her.

'You can have my rabbit if you like.' Kimiko held up the damp, bedraggled blue remains.

'Thank you, but I'm sure he would not like the hospital. He'll be happier with you.' Sister Elaine waved from the door.

The lounge was out of bounds, a marshy disaster. The children waited upstairs in the hidy-hole for the bus to arrive. A few of the older ones had been allowed down to the landing on the floor below. There Annette Rouleau sat huddled on the orange sofa, her make-up smeared and worn, her expression exhausted. At the sight of the children she drew back sullenly and stared without a word, puffing in short stabs on her last black Russian cigarette. The children settled on the last step of the landing and watched her silently.

'Do you feel better?' Mariko asked politely.

'Have your stomach pains gone?' said Yumiko.

'Yes, thank you,' Annette answered icily and immediately looked away, ignoring them. Mariko and Yuniko exchanged a glance under raised eyebrows. They shrugged and began to make comments about the past night. Annette drummed her fingers impatiently, waiting for the orphanage bus that would drop her, Dennis and Hartley back in Kobe on the way to Osaka. Hartley's parked car was a battered and waterlogged wreck.

In the hidy-hole Yoshiko Mori and Eiko Kubo attempted to keep the smaller girls and boys occupied. Eiko's cheeks were still a healthy red, undisturbed by the night, but Yoshiko was drained and white. Eiko looked at her worriedly.

'Why don't you sit down, I can manage here.'

'No, no. I'm quite all right,' Yoshiko answered.

'I can manage very well without you. I don't need you here,' Eiko replied.

'Well, really ...' Yoshiko said, affronted.

'I mean ... I only meant ... I'm worried about you, that's all,' Eiko said hastily, flustered.

'You always say the wrong thing, Eiko,' Yoshiko sighed.

'Now, right over left, through the hole, and now pull tight, that's it ...' Arthur guided Nobuo's fingers, tying the knot.

'Now me. Me,' Hiroshi insisted. Arthur nodded and gave the string to Hiroshi. His fat caterpillar fingers wriggled impatiently from the end of his plaster. He laboured through the knot, his tongue stuck out in concentration.

'Show us some more,' said Jun.

'All right, now this one's called a tom foot knot. Here's a half hitch and a running noose, and this is a figure eight.'

Arthur's fingers moved nimbly, winding patterns in the string. The children watched, absorbed, and then looked up in admiration.

'Can't we be Scouts, can't we?' Kenichi asked.

'I like those knots. I'd like to be a Scout,' Jiro considered carefully.

'Well, I am not sure you are all old enough. But you could be Cubs, I'm sure. There are enough of you to form your own pack. Yes, that's quite an idea, quite an idea.' Arthur repeated, the thought taking hold of him. For he found himself strangely loath to end the night and the company of these children. Their small appraising eyes and lack of guile, so different from the assertive self-consciousness of the older boys he was used to, touched something new within him. In the morning sun, the battered night behind them, he felt some new dimension alive in him. As if he had been given a gift. He knew it was the children. He remembered Ruriko's small fingers in his mouth, and his stiff response seemed already to belong to another life. Another life. His mind filled suddenly with the thought of Kyo again, but he pushed it down hard.

'I shall ask Dr Kraig. We shall do something about it. Yes indeed,' promised Arthur.

'Then we'll see you again. You'll show us more knots?' Hiroshi anxiously confirmed. Arthur nodded solemnly.

'Will you really come and visit us?' Emiko pushed herself forward before the boys to stand in front of Arthur. 'Can girls be Cubs, too?'

'No. I'm afraid not, but we'll see if we can arrange a Brownie pack,' Arthur deliberated.

'Good. Now Junko wants to show you her wind dance. He's ready, Junko. He's watching.' At Emiko's signal, Junko began to whirl madly across the room, and stopped before Eiko Kubo. Arthur clapped politely.

'I know he is very small, but will you show him a knot.

Please.' Tami came forward, Toshio in tow. 'He's been such a good boy, haven't you, Toshio?' Tami patted the boy's small head as she had seen the women do.

'Oh yes, yes. We mustn't forget him,' Arthur agreed, and took Toshio on his knee. 'But after this I must go down to help Mr Cooper. I shall come back up as soon as I can.'

'Are you sure this is what you want?' Daniel asked Akiko.

'Yes, but I cannot do it alone,' she said, opening the door of the room. He followed her in.

She lowered her eyes as she walked. At the bed she took a breath before looking down at her mother.

They had closed Kyo's eyes, the wild look was gone from her face. Cast up at last from her own emotions the compression of life diminished, like a weight removed. Her face was round and smooth in death and reflected only absence. There was a delicacy now, never seen before, risen from beneath.

Akiko stared without a word. Beside her Daniel waited, silent. After a while she nodded to him and turned to leave the room. By the door they saw Eva waiting.

'I'm glad you came to see her,' Eva said quietly. 'You must not remember her with hate, Akiko. Life gave her the wrong hand, it wasn't her fault entirely. I knew another side of her as well, long ago, before life completely strangled her. And in her own way, she wanted the best for you, otherwise she would not have left you with me. She could have left you anywhere, but she came back here from Tokyo, so that she might give you to me. And that is what you must remember.'

'Yes, I know,' Akiko whispered. Daniel put an arm about her and looked at Eva.

'I'm going to look after her. I want Akiko to come back to America with me,' Daniel ended quickly, flustered. He hoped his aunt would not disapprove. He had not meant to tell her now, like this.

But Eva only smiled gently and nodded. 'We'll talk of it later.'

Outside the room Daniel put a hand on Akiko's shoulder and turned her to him.

'Are you all right? Did you mind that I told her?'

'No.' Akiko smiled and shook her head. For already she felt past and future melt and dissolve their strengths within her.

'For the first time I feel ready for the future.' She took his hand and silently they left the room.

Inside, Eva stared at Kyo, her face sad and tired, then walked across to the window. It had happened as she hoped it would. In every way there would be a new life for Akiko, a future devoid of stigma. For it had always worried her, the future she saw in Japan for Akiko. When the child was small it had seemed enough to protect and to love; it had seemed that righted the wrong society had done the child and those others like her. But now Akiko must take her own place in society. Even with Eva's protection that place was diminished and second-best. What if something ever happened to herself, Eva thought? What then would be Akiko's position? It worried her deeply. To part with the child, to send her so far away, that would not be easy. But it was a small price to pay for all Akiko would gain. Eva's eyes misted with emotion.

She thought of the strange and terrible night that seemed to have settled so many issues beyond the taking of life. The morning was damp and clear before her, recreated from the night. The sun glittered on pools of trapped water, in the bay the sea was like a deep fresh bruise, dark and blue, the opposite shore and mountains of Wakayama loomed up distinct and near. Eva wiped tears from her eyes and sighed, filled with grateful relief. Through the window she saw Hiroshi steal out of the front door, into the swampy garden below. There was always a child in need. In her mind the river of life with its battered bits of driftwood flowed on and stopped for nothing. She turned from the window to go and retrieve Hiroshi.

Nate Cooper, Hartley and Dennis inspected the car in the garage. Their bent backs collected beneath the bonnet of Nate's new blue Mercedes. Behind the wheel Arthur Wilcox prepared to start the car.

'Okay. Try it once more, Arthur. Last time,' Nate's voice said from inside the bonnet. The car choked and guffawed and then fell silent.

'Nope. It's no good. She's not going to do it.' Nate Cooper stretched himself up and wiped grease from his hands on a rag.

Now he would have to add the car and Maud's coffin to the accounts of last night. The car would come under insurance, as would most of the rest. But was there any way, he wondered, to get a coffin off the tax?

Arthur got out of the car and shut the door. His mind was filled suddenly again with the thought of Kyo. He remembered the delicate look of her dead face, the peace he had seen in it there. In death he had hardly recognised her. In a strange, oblique way it seemed fitting that it had been himself who had embraced her at the end. For at least he had cared for her sincerely, and he knew there may not have been another like him. Knowing the callous start to her life it was the least he felt she deserved, whatever she had become. Kyo. He said the word silently for the last time, and felt a sudden tugging at his trouser leg. He looked down and found Hiroshi beside him.

'Yes lad, what do you want?'

'What's a carburettor?' asked Hiroshi.

Also by Meira Chand

The Bonsai Tree
ISBN: 978-981-4828-23-9
Liberal-minded heir to a traditional business empire, Jun Nagai brings his beautiful, intelligent English wife Kate Scott back to Japan after a whirlwind romance. A marriage his powerful and complex mother Itsuko naturally disapproves. While Jun is pulled between the two cultures, owing loyalty to both, Kate is thrown into an unfamiliar world. Stripped of all romantic illusions, she struggles to retain her individuality in a world where her role of a wife lies within strict social constructs.

The Gossamer Fly
ISBN: 978-981-4828-21-5
Confronted by an arrogant and manipulative new maid after her mother is sent back to England following a breakdown, Natsuko, a young girl of English-Japanese parentage, is thrust into a dark and sinister adult world, causing her to retreat into mounting isolation, confusion, fear and anger, leading to a dramatic conclusion in this emotionally charged story.

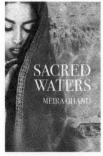

Sacred Waters

ISBN: 978-981-4779-50-0

Orphaned as a child and widowed at thirteen, Sita has always known the shame of being born female in Indian society. Her life constrained and shaped by the men around her, she could not be more different from her daughter, Amita, a headstrong university professor determined to live life on her own terms. Richly layered and beautifully evocative, the novel is a compelling exploration of two women's struggle to assert themselves in male-dominated societies of both the past and the present.

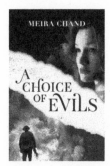

A Choice of Evils

ISBN: 978-981-4828-24-6

Set against the backdrop of the Sino-Japanese war of the 1930s, the story of those tumultuous years is told through the lives of a disparate group of fictional characters: a young Russian woman émigré caught between her complex love affair with a British journalist and a Japanese diplomat, an Indian nationalist working for Japanese intelligence, a Chinese professor with communist sympathies, an American missionary doctor and a Japanese soldier, all brought together by the monstrous dislocation of war, enmeshed in a savage world beyond their control.

ABOUT THE AUTHOR

Meira Chand is of Indian-Swiss parentage and was born and educated in London. She has lived for many years in Japan, and also in India. In 1997 she moved to Singapore, and is now a citizen of the country. Her multi-cultural heritage is reflected in her novels.

Also by Meira Chand:
A Different Sky
A Far Horizon
House of the Sun
The Painted Cage